PUFFIN BOOKS

# Always

Morris Gleitzman grew up in England and went to Australia when he was sixteen. He worked as a frozen chicken-thawer, sugar-mill rolling-stock unhooker, fashion-industry trainee, department-store Santa, TV producer, newspaper columnist and screenwriter. Then he had a wonderful experience. He wrote a novel for young people. Now he's one of our most popular children's authors. He lives in Melbourne, but visits Britain regularly. His many books include *Two Weeks with the Queen*, *Give Peas a Chance*, *Bumface*, *Boy Overboard* and the *Once* sequence of novels.

Visit Morris at his website:
morrisgleitzman.com

# Always

# MORRIS GLEITZMAN

PUFFIN

PUFFIN BOOKS

UK | USA | Canada | Ireland | Australia
India | New Zealand | South Africa

Puffin Books is part of the Penguin Random House group of companies
whose addresses can be found at global.penguinrandomhouse.com.

www.penguin.co.uk
www.puffin.co.uk
www.ladybird.co.uk

First published by Penguin Random House Australia Pty Ltd
and in Great Britain by Puffin Books 2021

001

Printed and bound in Great Britain by Clays Ltd, Elcograf S.p.A.

The authorized representative in the EEA is Penguin Random House Ireland,
Morrison Chambers, 32 Nassau Street, Dublin D02 YH68

A CIP catalogue record for this book is available from the British Library

ISBN: 978–0–241–38048–2

All correspondence to:
Puffin Books
Penguin Random House Children's
One Embassy Gardens, 8 Viaduct Gardens, London SW11 7BW

Penguin Random House is committed to a
sustainable future for our business, our readers
and our planet. This book is made from Forest
Stewardship Council® certified paper.

For all the children
who have now grown old
but are still young.

# Wassim

**Always** stay hopeful.

That's my motto.

You're probably thinking, he's such a dreamer, that Wassim. What's he got to be hopeful about? He's ten years old and look at his life.

Thanks, but it's not so bad.

I've got a lot to be hopeful about.

So has Uncle Otto.

I can't wait to tell him what I've just discovered at the public library. How it's going to make such a difference to our lives.

Mine and Uncle Otto's.

No more Iron Weasels threatening to hurt him if he can't get the parts to fix their cars. Or if he tells anyone about their crimes. Or if he tries to stop them making monkey noises at me.

Very soon Uncle Otto will be one of the most unthreatened people in Europe.

One of the happiest as well, most likely.

3

You're probably thinking, somebody tell Wassim he's just a kid. Ask him how much hope a kid like him has got of standing up to the Weasels. Has he forgotten they've got guns?

No, I haven't forgotten.

But I've still got a lot of hope.

Specially now there's a person who can help me.

A person who knows more than anyone about staying hopeful and dealing with vicious bullies.

A person called Felix Salinger.

**Always** be careful in public libraries.

They can be more dangerous than they look.

If you're lucky there'll be a librarian who's kind and helpful. Who says things like, 'Good morning, Wassim. How's the research going? Don't forget to wash your hands before you touch the books.'

But there might also be a senior librarian who gives you long suspicious stares because it's a week-day and you're not at school.

I'm where I've been all week, at a desk behind a shelf of history books and a big panel encouraging old people to use the library's 3-D printer.

I have to be very careful. If the senior librarian sees I'm here again, she might start making phone calls. And the police around here aren't very friendly to people like me.

It's worth the risk.

Public library computers are very good at helping you discover people's secret identities.

People like Felix Salinger.

I'm reading about his very incredible life.

His amazing childhood in Poland in World War Two. How he fooled the Nazis just by changing his name. How the Nazis wanted to kill him very much, but they weren't able to.

After the way he dealt with all that, I bet Felix Salinger will be able to help me and Uncle Otto with our problems standing on his head.

All I need to do now is find out how to get in touch with him.

I reach for the mouse.

But I don't click.

I freeze instead.

Behind me, a sound has started. A sound you hear a lot on TV, coming from crowds in football stadiums, specially here in Eastern Europe.

I also hear it up close sometimes. So close I can feel hot breath and blobs of spit on the back of my neck, that's how worked up the person is who's making the noises.

The monkey noises.

I jump up and turn round.

Two big teenagers. One still jibbering, the other one grinning. Both wearing Iron Weasels jackets.

'Whatcha doing, monkey boy?' says the grinner.

I don't answer.

What I want to say is, 'What's wrong with you lot? Just because you support a football team that's not much good, don't take it out on everyone else.

Bullying doesn't make a team better, you idiots.'

But I keep quiet.

Their dads are Iron Weasels too, and if you insult their team, some of the dads get their guns out.

The grinning teenager grabs me round the head. His arm is like a car wrecker's clamp, twisting my head into his armpit.

I catch sight of what the other one's doing. He's stopped making monkey noises and he's peering at the computer screen.

At the old photos in the newspaper article I was reading about Felix Salinger.

'Look at that,' he sniggers. 'Monkey boy's doing a school project on Nazis and Jews.'

I lunge towards the desk, trying to turn the computer off.

But I can't. The grinning Weasel clamps my head even tighter. It feels like it's being wrenched out of shape.

Doesn't matter. The article is in English, which I'm pretty sure these two thugs don't speak because they probably haven't got mothers who are as smart as mine was.

The other Weasel sees something on the desk and picks it up.

'*William Does His Bit*,' he mutters, staring at the cover of my Richmal Crompton book. 'Who said you could read about white people, jungle boy?'

'Put that down,' I say. 'It's not a library book. My grandpa left me that in his will.'

But the Weasel doesn't put it down. He sees what I'm using as a bookmark.

Grandpa Amon's secret note to me.

Which is not for anyone else to read.

The Weasel doesn't care about that. He grabs the note and reads it out loud.

'*Dear Wassim. Your life won't be easy. And I won't be there to help you. So if you're ever in big trouble, see a man called Wilhelm Nowak. He'll help you because of what I gave him at Speerkopf. Good luck, from Grandpa Amon.*'

The Weasels smirk at each other as if this is the funniest thing they've ever heard.

'What did he give him at Speerkopf, wherever that is?' says the Weasel who's crushing my head. 'A kiss?'

The Weasels both chortle.

I can't stand them being mean about Grandpa Amon, who died when I was three weeks old, but who I love very much.

'Put that note back,' I say. 'I only found it last week and I need it.'

I wish I was like Felix Salinger when he was young. I wish I had the fighting skills he learned from the partisan freedom fighters.

I don't have any fighting skills, but I'm desperate, so I give one of Felix's a try.

I twist my body, ignoring the pain, and jab my knee as hard as I can into the back of the head-crusher's knee.

He yells and half falls and I pull myself out of his grip, staggering backwards and crashing into a bookshelf.

The tall bookshelf begins to wobble.

It starts to fall.

I try to steady it.

Then I see both Weasels coming at me, faces pink with fury.

I let go of the shelves and jump sideways.

The bookshelf falls forward until it crashes against another bookshelf, which stops it.

But the history books don't stop. They hurtle off the shelves and smack hard into the Weasels, knocking them both off their feet.

Close by, a woman shouts something.

I grab my book and my note.

'You boys,' says the woman's voice, stern and furious. 'Leave this library immediately.'

The Weasels are both scrambling up, frantically brushing the books away as if they're poisonous.

The senior librarian is glaring at us. Next to her is the nice librarian, hands over her mouth with concern. The senior librarian holds up her phone. Which I think is official librarian language for *do what I say or I'll call the police.*

'Out,' she yells. 'Now.'

I do what she says. I duck past the Weasels and sprint towards the door and outside and across the carpark away from the library.

But not away from the Weasels.

I can hear them behind me, feet clumping, breath sucking.

Getting closer.

'Maybe the monkey boy's Jewish,' one of them pants loudly, like he wants me to hear it. 'Can you be black and Jewish?'

'Dunno,' says the other one. 'Get his willy out, that'll tell us.'

They're even closer.

I have to do something.

Suddenly I stop. And turn. And glare at them.

For a second I haven't got a clue what I'm doing. The Weasels don't either. They stop too, a bit startled, but still angry and violent.

I don't care. I'm bursting with the feelings I get when the Weasels, the grown-up ones, bully Uncle Otto. And mock him for looking after me.

'Change of plan,' I yell at the teenage Weasels in front of me. 'Things are different now.'

They stare at me.

'Your bullying days are over, Weasels,' I say. 'We've got Felix Salinger on our side now. He eats scum like you for breakfast.'

I glare at them.

They sneer at me, but I can see they're a bit uncertain. And puzzled. They probably haven't got a clue who Felix Salinger is.

Tough.

I'm not telling them anything else. Let them find out that Felix Salinger is the same person as the

Wilhelm Nowak in Grandpa Amon's secret message. If they can. I'm keeping Felix Salinger's details to myself for now. That's what you do with secret weapons.

'He must be one tough dude, this Felix Salinger,' growls one of the Weasels. 'Which he'll need to be.'

I know he will.

'Speerkopf,' says the other one. 'We'll check it out. See who this Felix Salinger is. Decide if we need to be scared.'

'Or,' says the first Weasel, 'if *you* do.'

They turn and walk away, both of them making loud monkey noises.

I walk in the other direction. Trying to swagger. But not finding it easy. My legs are trembling, and I'm starting to feel uncertain myself now.

I think I might have exaggerated about what Felix Salinger eats for breakfast.

He might prefer muesli.

I'm thinking he probably does, now I've just finished a slightly worrying calculation.

When Grandpa Amon met Wilhelm Nowak, who was actually Felix Salinger, at the Speerkopf Regional Nazi Command Centre in Poland in 1942, Felix Salinger was my age.

Which means that now he's eighty-seven.

**Always** try not to worry your parents.

That's my motto with Mum and Dad. Which is why, when I feel tears coming, I always do my best to have them before I get here.

Plus today, because it's been snowing, Mum will be worried about me catching a cold. So I'm making sure both my coat flaps are wrapped warmly round my legs as I kneel down next to her and Dad.

And gently brush the snow off their gravestone.

'Hi, Mum and Dad,' I say softly. 'I've got some really good news.'

It always feels weird whispering to them. But you have to in a cemetery. Talking loudly in a sad place can attract attention. You can end up being chased away by cemetery officials. Which is very upsetting for your parents when they're gone and they can't protect you.

'I've found him,' I whisper to Mum and Dad.

'I've found Wilhelm Nowak. The man Grandpa's note says will help us.'

I pause to let this sink in.

'His real name is Felix Salinger,' I say. 'He used to be Polish and now he lives in Australia. There's a whole long article about his life in a newspaper there. And the Australian government gave him a really high-up award for being such a brilliant surgeon.'

I pause again.

I don't mention Felix Salinger's age. When I'm telling Mum and Dad my news, I try to be honest and truthful, but also hopeful. So they can be hopeful too.

'A man like him,' I say, 'probably knows heaps of important people. So if he's feeling a bit too old and weary to help us with the Weasels, he's probably got loads of friends here in Europe who can do it instead. Important doctors, government ministers, army generals . . .'

A gentle breeze blows, just enough to lift the ear flaps of my beanie.

We don't get many gentle winter breezes around here, mostly storms and gales, so this is how I know Mum and Dad have heard me and are wishing me good luck.

'Thanks, Mum and Dad,' I whisper.

I've had heaps of good luck, thanks to them.

Last week, for example, when I found Grandpa Amon's secret message. That was my lucky day.

Mum and Dad are amazing, helping me with so much good luck after what happened to them.

No good luck for them at all.

I take a deep breath. Trying not to have tears.

I don't want to worry them.

Not now I'm so close to having the best luck of my life.

Which I'm hoping will happen tonight, after dinner, when me and Uncle Otto do the washing-up and then get in touch with Felix Salinger.

**Always** just trying to do their best, that's how most people are.

It was one of Mum's favourite mottos.

As I hurry through the darkness towards Uncle Otto's car-repair workshop, I can't help wishing it was one of Uncle Otto's mottos too.

It would make it easier for both of us when I'm late. He'd remember I've just been out trying to do my best, and he wouldn't get so cross and grumpy.

I'm not complaining.

I'm very lucky that Mum had Uncle Otto as her brother. Most of the time he's kind and loving, like her. I just wish he didn't get so stressed. It can't be good for him, when his head goes even more pink than usual.

I give the workshop door a push, but it's locked.

Then I hear footsteps thumping upstairs in the kitchen, which tells me Uncle Otto might be a bit cross and grumpy now.

If only I had a phone, I could have called him from the cemetery and told him about being late. But Uncle Otto doesn't think kids like me should have phones, because of unkind people online.

I find my key and open the door.

Uncle Otto's footsteps are still thumping.

The upstairs part of the workshop, where he lives, has a thick wooden floor.

But when Uncle Otto gets grumpy, he's so big and heavy the whole place shakes. Each time he has a girlfriend, they always complain about it.

I hurry up the stairs.

Uncle Otto is standing at the kitchen doorway, waiting. He looks at me with the expression he has a lot. Stressed and sad at the same time.

'Why d'you do this, Wassim?' he says. 'Why d'you make it so difficult?'

He turns and goes back to the stove.

I follow him in.

'Sorry, Uncle Otto,' I say. 'But I had to tell Mum and Dad about my research.'

Uncle Otto flips the pork chop over in the pan, slapping it down.

'Research for school?' he says.

'Better than that,' I say.

'What's better than school?' he says.

I hesitate. I always try to tell Uncle Otto the truth. But today I'd rather tell him the good news about Felix Salinger first, and then move on to the bad news about not being in class.

'They rang,' says Uncle Otto. 'I had a gearbox in pieces and the school rang again. Wanting to know where you were.'

'Sorry,' I say.

Uncle Otto hates being interrupted when he's working. He's a brilliant car mechanic and he works very hard to do the best job for his customers.

Even though some of them don't deserve it and should be in jail.

'I'm not a real parent,' says Uncle Otto. 'I haven't got the strong nerves of a real parent. So don't make me worry about you. How many times have I told you that?'

I don't reply.

We both know it's a lot.

Uncle Otto turns off the gas. He squeezes a big dollop of chilli sauce on to his chop as usual. Then he opens the cupboard door under the sink where the vegetable box is.

'I've got to do this,' he says. 'It's what a parent has to do.'

I know what's coming next. So I haven't got long to say what I need to say.

'I know where Wilhelm Nowak is,' I blurt out.

Uncle Otto turns and stares at me.

He saw Grandpa Amon's note last week when I found it hidden in my Richmal Crompton book. He said it was a very kind thought of Grandpa's, but I shouldn't get my hopes up because Wilhelm Nowak was probably lost in the mists of time.

'I know Wilhelm Nowak's real name,' I say. 'It's Doctor Felix Salinger. He lives in Australia. Their government gave him a medal. A newspaper did a big article about him.'

I keep on talking very fast, trying to fit in as much detail about Felix Salinger's life as I can while I have the chance.

Uncle Otto's face is getting the stressed and sad look again.

Mostly sad.

He holds up his hands, which means I have to stop talking.

'Wassim,' he says. 'Listen to me. Your grandpa loved you. Didn't matter he only knew you for a few weeks. But that note of his is two pistons short of a Daewoo. Think about it. Some kid a person shares a couple of books with back in the mists of time doesn't come helping seventy years later.'

You don't usually argue with Uncle Otto, but sometimes you have to.

'Felix Salinger remembers Grandpa Amon,' I say. 'Really well. He's very grateful to him. He says so in the newspaper.'

I hold out a piece of library toilet paper. On it is the link to the Australian newspaper article in my best handwriting. And a link to a website that'll translate the article for Uncle Otto.

Uncle Otto takes the piece of paper and tosses it on the table without looking at it.

Which makes me sad.

Next year is 2020. Uncle Otto turns fifty next year. A person deserves a really good present for their fiftieth birthday. Specially when they've been looking after a kid for eleven months and fifteen days who's not even their son.

But I can't afford to buy a really good present. So I'm giving him Felix Salinger instead.

'Please,' I say to Uncle Otto. 'Felix Salinger will help us, I know he will. And his friends will too. Imagine what that would be like, a Weasel-free life.'

Uncle Otto sighs and his shoulders sag.

For a moment I think he's going to agree.

But instead he snorts wearily.

'You're your mother's son,' he says. 'She was like you, stubborn as a rusted-on tube clamp. Coming back from England with a husband she knew would have a struggle fitting in here.'

I glare at Uncle Otto.

Sometimes he doesn't stick to the point.

'There's a big difference between what Mum did and what you're doing,' I say. 'Mum was in love with Dad, plus he was kind and generous and brave and funny. The Weasels are violent criminals.'

Uncle Otto doesn't like me saying things like that about the Weasels. And not just because he supports the same football team as them.

'They're my customers,' says Uncle Otto. 'I know they're not perfect, but I haven't got any choice. So stop dreaming about people from the past, Wassim. I'm here now and I look after you.'

Uncle Otto's shoulders sag again. They always do when he talks about how he hasn't got any choice.

He's right, he hasn't. Not at the moment.

But it doesn't always have to be like this.

I want to tell Uncle Otto not to lose hope, but he turns back to the cupboard under the sink and squats down and puts his head inside.

I wait while he finds what he's looking for.

When he's found it, he stands up, closes the cupboard and comes over.

And puts his arm round my shoulders.

Which he doesn't do very often, so I'm a bit surprised and speechless.

'Are you being bullied at school?' he says.

I think fast.

The last time Uncle Otto asked me about that, I told him the truth and he went to the school and threatened a lot of people. Not just kids.

I tell him the truth again.

But only about today. I wasn't bullied at school today because I wasn't there.

'No,' I say.

'Good,' he says. 'OK, you know the deal.'

I have to go to my room. It's the punishment Uncle Otto always gives me for skipping school.

But Uncle Otto's not a cruel person. He doesn't want me to starve. So when he sends me to bed without any dinner, he always gives me something from under the sink.

For basic nutrition.

He's holding something out to me now.

Tonight it's a carrot.

I flop on to my bed.

Carefully, because I don't want to damage it.

Uncle Otto built this bed for me with his own hands. He built this whole bedroom, using brand-new pieces of plywood and a new curtain.

Which was very kind, because it was a lot of hard work and trouble.

Fitting a whole new room into his workshop, even a small room like this, meant he had to shift a lot of tyres over against the wall. Plus brake linings and spark plugs and gear boxes and chemicals for flushing out engines that Uncle Otto says might explode if they get spilled.

And then a few weeks ago, he had to shift everything again when the Weasels made him store a huge pile of stolen iPads here.

I sigh and have a bite of my carrot.

I'm very lucky I've got this room. And Uncle Otto. Some kids have to live on the streets when their parents aren't around any more.

I switch on my lamp and pick up *William Does His Bit* by Richmal Crompton. Who, I learned at the library today, was also Felix Salinger's favourite author when he was a kid.

That must be how he met Grandpa Amon.

I stare at Grandpa Amon's note.

I feel sad that I only knew Grandpa Amon for three weeks and I can't even remember his face.

But I feel very happy that me and him are both giving Felix Salinger to Uncle Otto.

Tomorrow I'll go back to the library and use the creative thinking I got from Grandpa Amon and the determination I got from Mum and the hopefulness I got from Dad.

I'll use them to find out Felix Salinger's address, and then I'll contact him.

I must have fallen asleep reading, because when I open my eyes I've still got my coat on and there's cold dribble on my chin and my eyes are bleary.

But my ears are working.

They're full of the sound I hate the most.

Big old Mercedes cars roaring across the waste ground outside the workshop and stopping right in front of our side entrance.

Car doors slamming. Like my chest is now.

I haven't got a clue what the time is.

Late, probably.

They don't care about that. They never do.

The Iron Weasels.

**Always** have a glass of water in your hand.

That way, if people see you out of your room when you shouldn't be, specially violent thugs, at least you've got an excuse.

I read that motto in a story.

This is the first time I've used it.

I tiptoe up the workshop stairs, trying to hear what the Iron Weasels are saying to Uncle Otto in his office. Their gruff voices are angry but muffled. Some of the Weasels are even bigger than Uncle Otto, and I can hear their thumping feet even on the shag-pile office carpet Uncle Otto bought from someone in a pub.

At the top of the stairs I duck into the kitchen and half fill a glass with water, slowly so the pipes don't bang. Then I creep along the dark hallway to the office door.

It's closed, but I can still hear better up here.

A voice is speaking.

I haven't heard this voice before.

It's not gruff like the others. It's more sort of grating and whiny. Like when a crankshaft is doing damage to an engine.

'Last warning, Kurtz,' the voice says in Polish. 'Here's what'll happen the next time that little jungle vermin of yours sticks his nose where it doesn't belong and shoots his mouth off. We'll find someone else to fix our cars. Then we'll fix you.'

I feel sick. I should have warned Uncle Otto that I'd yelled at some teenage Weasels.

Another voice replies, mumbling.

It's Uncle Otto, but I can't hear what he's saying.

I hate it when they threaten Uncle Otto. And I hate how he has to take it because there's always more of them than there is of him.

I wish I was bigger.

And armed.

But I'm not, so I keep quiet.

On the other side of the door, the crankshaft Weasel is speaking again.

'We're losing patience with you, Kurtz,' he says. 'If you've got a problem doing what we tell you, remind yourself what a cruel and unlucky place the world is. And how there's one person in your family who hasn't been unlucky. So far.'

Uncle Otto mutters something.

There's the sound of a slap. And a yelp. I've never heard Uncle Otto yelp before, but I know it was him.

In pain.

I bang the door open.

'Stop doing that,' I yell. 'It's not his fault. Those teenagers at the library started it. You can't punish Uncle Otto for something he didn't do. It's not fair.'

That's all I get to say.

Big hands grab me round the throat.

And squeeze. Hard.

I can't breathe. My neck is being crushed. The room is going wobbly.

Faces all around me are glaring and sneering. Uncle Otto is looking horrified.

I can't help it, I drop my glass of water on to the floor. Then I'm on the floor too, gasping.

Uncle Otto is crouching over me, his eyes wide and frantic.

'Wassim,' he says, gently massaging my neck.

'It's OK,' I croak. 'I'm OK.'

Two of the Weasels try to drag Uncle Otto away from me. He doesn't let them. I can see they're about to get more violent.

I manage to take a deep breath.

'See,' I say to Uncle Otto. 'I can breathe. It's OK. Don't worry.'

'Enough of this,' says the crankshaft voice, cross and irritable. 'Back to business.'

The Weasels pull Uncle Otto to his feet, but then they let go of him.

'Go back to bed,' Uncle Otto says to me, his face showing how much he means it. 'Now.'

Before anyone can throttle me again, or hurt Uncle Otto, I scramble up and sprint to the stairs and run down to my room.

I dive under the bedcovers, my heart going on all eight cylinders like Dad's was once after he helped Uncle Otto lift an engine block into a car.

Nobody comes down.

Not Uncle Otto or an angry Weasel.

I check my neck. It's sore, but I think it's OK. I must have a strong neck. It always survives when bullies at school try to crush it too.

My heart is still on high revs. But I'm getting used to breathing again. And I'm listening to what's going on upstairs.

More talking. Some shouting.

I can hear the different voices, but I can't hear what they're saying.

The loudest voice is the one in my head.

The whiny crankshaft voice from before.

Making threats about how unlucky our family has been. Me and Mum and Dad.

But not Uncle Otto.

So far.

Soon the Weasels leave.

Car doors slamming, big engines roaring, slush and dirt spraying against the outside wall of the workshop as they speed away.

Gone. For now.

I wait for Uncle Otto to come down.

He doesn't.

I listen for his footsteps moving around upstairs. Silence.

Perhaps he's having a glass of vodka to calm his nerves before bed. He says it's good to have when you're upset, and saves you cleaning your teeth.

I wait. Still no footsteps. No clang of an empty vodka bottle being dropped into the rubbish bin in the bathroom.

I have a thought I can't get rid of.

A terrible one.

Perhaps that wasn't just shouting I heard earlier. Perhaps it was more violence.

I dash out of my room and up the stairs.

Uncle Otto's office door is open.

In the dark hallway, yellow light from the office gleams on wet footprints. The Weasels must have made them as they left.

I can't tell if the wetness is from the water I spilled, or from something much worse that the Weasels spilled.

I run to the office doorway and peer in.

Uncle Otto is sitting at his desk with his back to me. Hunched forward, not moving.

For a moment I panic. Then Uncle Otto picks up the half-empty bottle at his elbow and fills his vodka glass and drinks.

I wait for my breathing to slow down before I speak to him. I'm not even sure what I'll say. Doesn't matter, I just want to check he's OK.

Then I see that Uncle Otto is looking at something on his computer. I can't make out any details, except for one big word at the top of the screen.

The name of the newspaper in Australia.

Uncle Otto must be reading the article about Felix Salinger.

'Uncle Otto,' I say.

Uncle Otto jolts in his chair and spills some vodka and spins round and stares at me.

I don't let his startled and grumpy expression put me off.

'I'm sorry,' I say. 'I should have told you about the teenage Weasels.'

Uncle Otto sighs.

He comes over to me and gently touches my neck again, peering at it.

'I'm sorry too,' he says. 'I was coming down to see you, but I had to check something first.'

'It's OK,' I say. 'I'm fine.'

Which I am, now I've seen what he's reading.

'You're a brave kid,' says Uncle Otto. 'But please, Wassim, learn when to keep your mouth shut. For your own sake.'

I don't say anything.

I don't want to distract Uncle Otto any more from the research I hope he'll do very soon.

Research to find Felix Salinger's contact details so we can ask for help. Before the Weasels lose their patience and hurt Uncle Otto a lot and make him unlucky too.

Uncle Otto doesn't say anything either.

He looks at me for a long time.

His face is almost as sad and stressed as it was after Mum and Dad died.

'Go back to bed,' he says.

I start to turn away, but Uncle Otto puts his hand on my shoulder.

'I promise you, Wassim,' he says. 'Those scum will never lay another finger on you, ever.'

'Or on you,' I say. 'That's a promise too.'

I don't say who will make this promise come true. I don't need to.

Uncle Otto knows.

**Always** sit in the front carriage if you're on a train and you need to have a private conversation.

Specially a conversation that could include an uncle getting cross.

This front carriage is almost empty.

Which is good for me and Uncle Otto.

We need to talk.

Since we left home this morning, Uncle Otto has said about eight words. Just asked me a couple of times if my neck's OK. When I tell him it's fine, he nods and goes back to being sad and silent again.

I'm worried about him. It's been more than a day since we've had a conversation. Yesterday was Saturday, and we didn't even talk about football.

OK, he was very busy on the phone in his office. He even got me to cook our pork chops for lunch, which he's never done before.

'Uncle Otto,' I said as we ate them, 'can I help you do whatever it is you're doing?'

I hoped he was trying to get in touch with Felix Salinger.

Uncle Otto gave me a sad look.

'I can manage, thanks,' he said. 'I'm just making arrangements for us to go somewhere safe.'

I opened my mouth to ask a million more questions, but Uncle Otto just pointed to my mouth and then at my chop.

'Eat,' he said. 'No time for talk.'

Well, we've got time to talk now.

'Uncle Otto,' I say.

He's staring out the train window at the roads and the traffic.

We hardly ever catch a train, and never in this direction out of town, so he's probably interested in what cars people drive in these parts and how well repaired they are.

'This safe place we're going to,' I say. 'You don't have to tell me where if that's a secret. But does it have good wi-fi?'

Not for Netflix, I'm about to say. For contacting Felix Salinger.

Uncle Otto turns to me.

Still looking sad.

'Please, Wassim,' he says. 'Trust me.'

He stares out the window again.

Uncle Otto isn't a big fan of conversation, but we usually talk more than this.

It must be stress and I think I know why.

Yesterday, a stranger with a van turned up late in the afternoon and loaded about a hundred of the Weasels' iPads into it and gave Uncle Otto a bundle of money.

I wasn't meant to see, but I did.

Afterwards I asked Uncle Otto if the Weasels had given him permission to sell the iPads, but he wouldn't answer.

He just sighed in a cross way and said, 'Please, Wassim, trust me,' and sent me to my room without a vegetable, which I think meant the answer was no.

The way Uncle Otto is staring out of the train window again now, I can see he's trying to tell me this conversation is over too.

His hands are showing it isn't.

They're gripping each other. His knuckles are white with stress, and his arm muscles under his Iron Weasels tattoos are bulging with stress as well.

I can't stay silent.

We're a family, me and him.

When somebody in a family is sad because he might never see his car workshop ever again, and stressed because his life could be in danger from selling iPads, the rest of the family should show how much they care and want him to be OK. That's one of the reasons talking was invented.

'Uncle Otto,' I say. 'When we get wherever we're going, I think we should get in touch with Felix Salinger straight away and ask for his help.'

Uncle Otto looks at me again.

32

He nods.

I feel a big surge of relief.

That's the thing about Uncle Otto. When he looks at you and nods, you know he means it.

It feels so much better now, sitting on this train with him. Imagining where we're going.

To a secret safe place in the countryside that the Weasels don't know about. With a really good internet connection so we can have a long Skype with Felix Salinger.

Uncle Otto is so clever deciding to get us there by train. His car can be a bit of a security risk.

It's a yellow 1969 V8 Chevy Camaro with orange speed stripes, so it's quite hard to go anywhere in it without being noticed.

I look at Uncle Otto.

'Thanks for being such a good uncle,' I say.

He looks at me.

Gentle and sad at the same time.

So sad that I think for a moment he might be having tears.

'I wish we didn't have to do this,' he says. 'I wish I could do what I promised at the funeral. Look after you. Just me.'

'You do look after me,' I say. 'Heaps. But it's like what Mum and Dad used to say those times we came over to give you a hand with your housework and your bottle recycling. Nobody can do it all on their own.'

Uncle Otto wipes his eyes.

I wish this train carriage was packed.

Full of people who'd normally be nervous at the size of Uncle Otto's knuckles and tattoos. So they could see how sensitive and caring he really is.

'One day you'll understand,' says Uncle Otto.

'I do understand,' I say. 'We're doing this to get away from the Weasels so they can't lose patience and hurt you ever again.'

Uncle Otto looks at me.

'Oh, Wassim,' he says sadly. 'It's not just me that they'd hurt.'

I stare at him, confused.

Uncle Otto reaches out and for a second I'm worried he's going to loosen my scarf.

I don't want him to see what's underneath.

The bruises on my neck.

I'm worried if he does, he'll take me to a doctor instead of to a secret hiding place with good wi-fi.

But he doesn't touch my scarf.

He just holds my hands in his.

I look at our hands, his big rough pink ones and my smaller brown ones, and suddenly I understand exactly what's been going on.

All the Weasel nastiness and bullying that Uncle Otto has been putting up with.

It's to protect me.

'I meant what I said,' Uncle Otto says quietly. 'I won't let them touch you again. We both won't. Me and Felix Salinger.'

I open my mouth to thank him.

With all my heart. In all the languages I learned from Mum and Dad.

Which usually makes him smile.

But before I can, something outside the window of the train makes me go silent.

We're stopping at a station.

It says *AIRPORT*.

Uncle Otto reaches into his coat pocket and pushes something into my hands.

I look at it.

I know exactly what it is.

Mum got it for me so I'd have something to shut bullies up when they tell me I can't be from this country because I'm the wrong colour.

I was emotional when she gave it to me, very emotional, but not as emotional as I am now to be holding it here.

And to see that Uncle Otto is holding his too.

Our passports.

# Felix

**Always** in my heart.

I say it louder than I normally would because of all the noise around us.

People clattering past give us a look.

Doesn't matter.

If you can't tell your granddaughter how much you love her at an international airport departure gate, where can you say it?

Zel's eyes are soft with emotion.

'Thank you, Felix,' she says. 'I know that. I always have. Every day I'm over there in Syria, you'll be in my heart too.'

We squeeze hands.

'Expect random texts,' says Zel, 'reminding you of that. Or, if the mobile signal in those war-zone hospitals is as bad as Mum and Dad say, telepathic messages.'

Zel grins.

I do too.

'I'll be whooping with joy,' I say. 'Either way. Even here in drizzly Melbourne.'

There's so much else I could say to her.

How much I'll miss her. How scared I am that I'll never see her again.

But I don't.

This is her day. This brave young woman with her loving smile. Calm, even in this overexcited crowd with their even more overexcited luggage trolleys.

'I'm so proud of you, Zel,' I say. 'All that work you put into Year Twelve, and now this. In a few years you're going to be a wonderful doctor.'

Zel looks serious again.

'If I do ever manage that,' she says, 'it'll mostly be because of you, Felix.'

She hugs me.

'And in return,' she says, 'I'm not going to give you any farewell lectures. I'm not going to remind you about your life. How much you've done for other people. How much you've given to the future. How this is your time now, to enjoy your own future. To relax and read heaps of books and eat too many toasted cheese sandwiches. I'm not going to say any of that.'

She tries to grin again.

But I can see in her dear earnest face how much she really does want all those things for me. I do as well, but, oh, Zel, if only it was that simple.

I give her a smile that I hope is reassuring.

'Look at me,' I say. 'Retired and happy. Devoted member of eleven libraries. Healthy and content.'

All of which is true.

Sort of.

'You are a dope,' says Zel through her tears.

I put my arms round her and we hug again.

'Stay safe, dear Zel,' I whisper to her.

'I'll try,' she says.

She steps back and looks at me with such love.

'Take it easy, dear dopey Felix,' she says.

I hesitate, but only for a moment.

'I'll try,' I say.


Soon it's time.

We swap a few quick last words as we walk to the Passengers Only gate.

Zel promises to be back to start uni in fourteen months. I remind her to tell her dad when she gets to Syria to call me whenever he likes.

'He already knows that,' says Zel sadly.

I nod.

'You know how he is,' she says.

She gives me a sympathetic look and we share a last hug. A long one. Then she's gone.

I send her a quick telepathic message.

*Find someone nice to watch your back.*

I wipe my eyes and head to the carpark.


Halfway down the escalator, a woman's voice starts yelling excitedly behind me.

'Doctor Salinger! Doctor Salinger!'

I turn. Struggling down the steps towards me, squeezing past bewildered people, is a woman in her forties wearing an airline uniform.

'Doctor Salinger,' she calls. 'It's me, Sheree Nile. Remember?'

I look at her.

I don't remember. But I'm hoping I will in the next few seconds.

'This is Doctor Felix Salinger,' the woman says loudly to the people on the escalator as they let her through. 'When I was eight I got a twisted bowel and it perforated and the whole thing went septic. I was a goner, pus and blood pouring out of me. But Doctor Salinger didn't give up. He operated for eight hours.'

I do remember.

Sheree reaches me and gives me a big hug.

'This man saved my life,' she says. 'Doctor Felix Salinger. A hero. A national living treasure.'

We're at the bottom of the escalator now, in the Arrivals Hall. People are staring, wondering what the commotion is.

Sheree Nile tells them all, loudly.

'Doctor Felix Salinger,' she says several times.

Most of the people are looking puzzled, or amused, or mildly disapproving.

But not two men with shaved heads and football shirts. Their stares are different, eyes narrowed in a very unfriendly way.

Not at Sheree.

Just at me.

I tell myself that maybe they've been arrested in the past for creating a disturbance in a public place and they're resentful I'm getting away with it.

Or something.

Sheree has grabbed my hands and is squeezing them, beaming at me.

'What a coincidence seeing you,' she says. 'My doctor was telling me only last week about you giving all your money to the Children's Hospital. You're an angel.'

'Thank you,' I say. 'But even doctors exaggerate a bit sometimes. It's good to see you, Sheree. Is everything OK? Everything still working?'

'Like clockwork,' says Sheree.

'I'm happy to hear that,' I say.

She stops squeezing my hands and holds them gently, peering at them, concerned.

'Sorry,' I say. 'Bit shaky these days. Mostly with excitement when I hear a patient's doing well.'

Sheree looks at me.

'Doctor Salinger,' she says, 'if you're ever back here and you need help with anything, luggage or boarding or anything, you just let me know. It would be my honour to see you right.'

What a lovely person.

'That's very kind,' I say. 'Thank you.'

'I'd better get back to the check-in counter,' says Sheree. 'This has made my day. Bless you.'

We wave as she goes up the escalator.

Then I glance around.

The people who were staring have moved on. Including, I'm relieved to see, the two disgruntled soccer fans.

I make my way slowly towards the carpark, thinking about Sheree and how lucky I've been to have patients like her.

Which should leave me with a spring in my step. Or at least in my walking stick.

But it hasn't really.

Not Sheree's fault.

Those two men in football shirts. The way they were looking at me. I've no idea why, nothing to do with me probably, but it's left dark shadows lurking at the back of my mind.

If Zel's right, if my life's work is over, if there's no more giving to the future, so be it.

I've still got my books and my dog and all my own teeth.

But it does seem a bit unfair. No longer being able to use the wonderful things I was given as a child. The love and inspiration and opportunities. And yet still having to live with the dark shadows of everything that was taken away.

**Always** hopeful.

That's how I used to be.

Jumble still is.

Look at him. Whatever it was he just heard has made him hysterical with hope. Barking, wheezing, skittering across the kitchen mat, jamming his nose under the back door, rear end a blur.

If he's not careful, he'll need an anterior cruciate tail reconstruction.

'Jumble, please,' I say. 'Calm down. Have some breakfast. There's nobody out there to play with. It's four thirty in the morning.'

Jumble gives me an indignant frown.

Speak for yourself, his look says. I know we're both old and one of us suffers from a leg-related sleeping disorder, but we can still be hopeful. Get a life, Felix.

I smile. But only for a moment.

Another noise outside.

One I hear this time. A plant pot breaking.

Somebody in the backyard.

Jumble is barking again. I ask him to shush so I can listen. He gives my hand a nervous lick. He's having second thoughts about horizon-expanding social opportunities.

Whoever's out there has gone silent.

I stand up and creep over to the window, trying to keep the snap, crackle and pop in my knees as quiet as possible.

I give my glasses a wipe and peek out.

Just shadowy bushes. Moonlight on the lawn. And a backpack I don't think I've ever seen before, hanging from the half-open door of the shed.

A door that shouldn't be open at all.

I remember something I read recently. About desperate homeless people sleeping in Melbourne backyard sheds. At least it's not cold this time of year. But they'd still be needing a hot meal.

I go to the kitchen bench and switch on the sandwich toaster, just in case.

Then I hear Zel's voice.

Granddaughters can do that when you haven't got used to them being gone. Even when they're thousands of kilometres away, scrubbing up in Syria, hard at work with their parents. They can send a telepathic message whenever they feel like it. Saying things like, *Felix, please. Don't push your luck. It could be a cannibal zombie psychopath out there. Call the police.*

I sigh.

Nearly three days and I'm missing her more, not less. I'm missing the amused look she'd have on her face right now. After I told her that cannibal zombie psychopaths probably like toasted cheese sandwiches even more than human flesh.

Zel would argue about that, of course.

I'm going to miss our arguments so much.

Nothing makes you feel more hopeful about the future than watching a young person, eyes lit up, out-thinking an old one.

Even when the old one's you.

A violent noise shatters my thoughts.

Somebody thumping hard and loud, over and over, on the back door.

Jumble makes a hurried retreat under the table, scowling and barking.

'It's OK,' I say to him gently. 'If it's a zombie I'll call the police.'

The thumping continues, getting even louder, and a voice calls out.

I blink with surprise.

Did I hear what I thought I just heard?

Hard to know for sure with so much thumping and barking going on.

I tell Jumble to shush and he switches to a loud wheeze.

The thumping stops.

The voice calls out again, yelling my name again, high-pitched and urgent.

I don't recognise the voice.

But I did hear right the first time.

It's not a desperate hungry homeless person out there, or a cannibal zombie psychopath.

It's a child.

**Always** children.

That's one of the most painful things a doctor has to learn. Always children among the casualties.

It's a miracle so many doctors stay hopeful.

And so many children.

The boy standing outside my kitchen door is very hopeful. I don't know him, but even before the back door is fully open I see how hopeful he is.

'Are you Felix Salinger?' he says.

'Yes,' I say, trying to stay hopeful myself. 'Has something happened? Are you OK?'

The boy is about ten, jiggling with energy. His face is glowing with it and a bit of perspiration from the early-morning summer humidity.

Not surprising. He's clutching a heavy winter coat. And he's wearing a thick scarf.

'The Felix Salinger who tried to blow up a Nazi headquarters?' says the boy. 'When you were a kid?'

I look at him, surprised.

'That's right,' I say.

'In 1942?' says the boy. 'The Speerkopf Regional Nazi Command Centre. That one?'

'Yes,' I say. 'That one.'

His energy is making me smile. But I try not to show it in case something bad has happened.

I'm hoping he just wants help with a school project. A few local students have turned up here with their history projects. But never this early in the morning. And not speaking a mixture of English and Polish.

'Sorry about all the questions, Felix Salinger,' says the boy. 'And the yelling. I needed to check that it was you. I wasn't sure. The library computer said you're very eminent and well respected, so I thought your house would be bigger.'

This time I can't stop myself smiling.

'I'm very glad you are you,' says the boy. 'I was begging the library not to let me down. Because I need you to be you.'

He pulls a tattered book from his coat pocket.

I stare at it.

It's an old Polish copy of *William Does His Bit* by Richmal Crompton. My favourite author when I was a kid. And it looks like she's still being read in our Polish community.

'My grandpa left me this in his will,' says the boy. 'It's good, but it's taking me ages because I'm fast at speaking Polish, but slow at reading it. Then last week I was helping Uncle Otto with a noisy muffler and I dropped a rust scraper on the cover and it got ripped. I'm a bit clumsy sometimes. Sorry about your pot plant.'

I see that the spine of the book is damaged.

The boy is pulling something out of a jagged tear in it. A creased and slightly grubby piece of paper, folded tightly into a long strip.

'This was hidden inside,' says the boy. 'I didn't know it was there.'

He hands it to me.

I unfold it.

Wobbly handwriting, in Polish.

*Dear Wassim,*
*Your life won't be easy. And I won't be there to help you. So if you're ever in big trouble, see a man called Wilhelm Nowak. He'll help you because of what I gave him at Speerkopf.*
                    *Good luck, from Grandpa Amon*

I stare at the words.

Memories and emotions from a long time ago churning inside me.

Wilhelm Nowak, my wartime good-protection name in Poland when I was a kid.

Amon Kurtz, the Hitler Youth boy who offered friendship to a Jewish boy because we both loved the same books.

And now this visitor on my doorstep.

'Was Amon Kurtz your grandpa?' I say to the jiggling boy.

'Yes,' he says.

He's been watching me anxiously ever since I took the letter. Now he holds something else out to me. A passport, open at the photo page. The photo is him, a bit younger.

Wassim Kurtz.

Incredible.

And for a second a bit confusing.

Wassim is still speaking a mixture of English and Polish, but this passport isn't either of those.

Wassim notices me looking curious.

'It's a different country to Mum and Dad and Uncle Otto's passports,' he says. 'Our family had to move before I was born.'

I don't ask why.

Seeing Wassim, I think I can guess.

'Did your Grandpa Amon move too?' I say.

Wassim nods sadly.

'But I didn't really get to know him,' he says. 'Grandpa Amon died very soon after I was born. Uncle Otto taught me Polish, so we could speak it together and remember him.'

'I understand,' I say.

But there is something else that makes me curious and even a little puzzled.

Amon Kurtz had blond hair and blue eyes and pale skin. Wassim doesn't have any of those things.

But why should he?

Our genes are the most adventurous parts of us. Thanks to them we live in a world of wonderful possibilities as well as terrible ones.

I hold out my hand.

'I'm very happy to meet you, Wassim,' I say.

He looks up, hopeful again and a bit shy.

'I'm happy to meet you too,' he says, and we shake hands.

Then his smile fades, and so does mine.

'Wassim,' I say, 'Grandpa Amon's note says for you to find me if you're ever in trouble. Are you in trouble?'

Wassim nods.

'Quite a lot,' he says. 'But not as much trouble as Uncle Otto. That's why we both came from Eastern Europe to see you.'

I stare at him, taking this in.

Trying to imagine just how seriously in trouble you'd have to be to make a twenty-four-hour trip to see somebody you don't even know.

*Very*, says Wassim's face.

'Is your Uncle Otto here now?' I say, peering towards the shed.

Wassim's shoulders sag, all his hopeful energy suddenly gone.

He fumbles in one of his coat pockets and hands me another piece of paper. Not small and folded like Amon's. Bigger and crumpled.

Another handwritten message, in Polish again.

This one hastily scrawled.

WASSIM, I'M SORRY. STAY IN
AUSTRALIA WITH DR SALINGER.
I'M GOING BACK TO DO WHAT I
SHOULD HAVE DONE A LONG TIME
AGO.
  DOC, WASSIM IS A BRAVE BOY.
PLEASE TAKE CARE OF HIM.
                    UNCLE OTTO

Scrawled at the bottom is my address.

I stare at the page, shocked.

'I was asleep in the motel,' says Wassim, voice small and miserable. 'I woke up and Uncle Otto had gone. With his bag.'

I turn the piece of paper over.

On the other side is a printed airline itinerary showing flight details. An adult and a child coming from Eastern Europe to Australia.

Otto Kurtz and Wassim Kurtz.

Arriving yesterday.

Below it are details of a return flight booked for today. A flight that left three hours ago. Same two travellers. Except one of them is standing here in my backyard.

'If Uncle Otto had planned this,' says Wassim tearfully, 'why did he get me a return ticket?'

'He had to,' I say gently. 'They won't let you enter on a tourist visa without one.'

I'm not sure that makes poor Wassim feel any better.

He takes a deep breath.

'We came to ask for your help with the Iron Weasels,' says Wassim. 'I think Uncle Otto has gone back to try to deal with them on his own. Which means he's in really big danger. He sold some of their iPads.'

I stare at Wassim as I try to take this in.

Wassim struggles to keep his tears under control.

Poor kid.

Even though I don't have a clue what this is about, I can see he's a brave boy with far too much on his shoulders.

I give him a reassuring smile.

It won't help him to see an old man worrying about him. Or making him answer more questions on a doorstep.

'Why don't you come in,' I say. 'I was about to have breakfast. When I worked at a hospital, we solved all our problems while we had breakfast. Do you like toasted cheese sandwiches?'

'**Always** be careful around dogs,' says Wassim. 'That's what my mother used to tell me.'

He's staying a few steps behind me as we come into the kitchen.

Jumble is still under the table, peering out and growling suspiciously at Wassim.

'Jumble won't hurt you,' I say. 'He's getting a bit old. New visitors make him nervous when he can't remember where he put his glasses.'

Wassim doesn't smile.

He looks like a boy who's been taught that dogs are no joke.

'Make yourself at home,' I say. 'Hang your bag and coat here and have a seat. Are you hungry?'

Wassim gives a small nod and sits at the table, pulling his scarf tighter around his neck.

He looks nervously at Jumble sprawled on the floor. Jumble drags himself to his feet and licks Wassim's hand.

Wassim pulls his hand away. Then cautiously holds it out for Jumble to lick again.

I smile to myself for both their sakes.

Before we eat, Wassim asks if he can use my phone to ring Uncle Otto.

'Of course,' I say. 'But if he's in flight, he'll have his phone switched off.'

'He might not be in flight,' says Wassim. 'He might have stopped for a drink on the way to the airport and missed the plane.'

I let Wassim ring.

From his face I see there's no answer.

'Leave a message,' I say.

Wassim frowns as he thinks of one.

'Uncle Otto,' he says. 'It's me. Please, don't do anything to make the Weasels upset. When you hear this message, call Felix Salinger's number.'

Wassim looks at me and I tell him the number and he repeats it into the phone.

'Please, Uncle Otto,' he says. 'Be sensible. Like you told me to be when I wanted to chuck out that rust scraper that damaged my book.'

Miserably, he hangs up.

I slide his plate across the table.

'Toasted cheese sandwich,' I say. 'Best medicine for disappointment.'

'Thanks,' says Wassim, and takes a bite. But I can see his mind's not really on toast or cheese.

'Uncle Otto's phone could just be flat,' he says.

'Him not answering doesn't definitely mean he's on the plane.'

'We could find out,' I say. 'If you want to.'

Wassim looks at me.

'In movies,' he says, 'they always say they won't give out that kind of information.'

'A kind ex-patient of mine works at the airport,' I say. 'I can ask her to do me a favour.'

Wassim thinks about this as he chews.

I can see how he's torn between wanting me to, and fearing what the answer will be.

'It's just information,' I say gently. 'It's what we do with it that counts.'

Wassim thinks some more, then his frown goes.

'That's a good motto,' he says. 'Thank you.'

I let Wassim eat for a bit, then ask him to tell me about where he lives, which he does.

'Uncle Otto says it's better for me than all the other places my family came from,' says Wassim. 'Germany and Poland and England and Africa.'

I can't imagine it's that much better for people like Wassim, but I don't say anything.

Wassim frowns again.

'Better,' he says, 'except for the Iron Weasels. Who aren't better in any way. They do a lot of bad things. At football matches and other places.'

Sometimes I watch the TV news from Eastern Europe, but I've never heard of the Iron Weasels.

I wish Wassim hadn't either, as I listen to the way they treat him and his Uncle Otto.

'Tell me about Uncle Otto,' I say.

'I think he's had enough of the Weasels,' says Wassim. 'I think he's decided to have a war with them. He thinks he can win it on his own but he can't. He's big and tough, but underneath he's very gentle. Eleven months and twenty days ago, when he started looking after me, he built me a bedroom at his place totally out of the goodness of his heart and new plywood.'

'And do you think he brought you to Australia,' I say, 'so you won't get hurt in his war?'

Wassim nods unhappily.

I consider this.

Even if all of Wassim's love and concern for Uncle Otto are making him exaggerate a bit, it still doesn't sound good.

Plus, when a boy is living with his uncle, there's a difficult question that needs to be asked.

'Wassim,' I say gently. 'Has something happened to your parents?'

Wassim looks at the floor.

He holds his hand out to Jumble, who drags himself up again and licks it.

'Uncle Otto is in so much serious danger,' says Wassim, 'I think we should just talk about Uncle Otto for now.'

'Fair enough,' I say.

There's another question I need to ask Wassim. I have a feeling it won't be an easy one for him to answer either.

'With everything that's going on,' I say, 'have you thought about talking to the police?'

Wassim jumps up, horrified.

His chair crashes over.

Jumble goes back under the table.

'No,' Wassim says. 'Not the police. That would be the worst possible thing.'

I try to explain to Wassim that in Australia a boy with brown skin doesn't have to fear the police like he might in Eastern Europe.

Not most of the time, anyway.

Wassim, still looking panicked, interrupts.

'Don't you understand?' he says. 'Uncle Otto has told me I must never, ever talk to the police.'

I look at him, not fully understanding.

'The minute we talk to the police,' says Wassim, 'Uncle Otto would be dead. The Weasels would know. Some of them are police.'

I sigh.

I've lived in this lucky country for too long.

'Sorry,' I say. 'I understand now.'

I start to explain that talking to the police here would be different, but Wassim interrupts again.

'That's the reason we need somebody else to help us,' he says. 'Somebody like you.'


After we finish our toasted sandwiches, Wassim insists on washing up.

'I always do it at home,' he says. 'I wash, Uncle Otto dries.'

I dry. Wassim keeps glancing at me. He seems to approve of my drying-up ability.

'You can take your scarf off if you're too hot,' I say to him. 'Jumble won't eat it.'

'I'm fine, thanks,' he says.

I understand this too. When I did my first week as a junior hospital intern, I was so stressed and anxious, I had some lucky socks I never took off.

Wassim tells me more about the Weasels. Their guns. Their stolen iPads. What they're likely to do with the guns when they discover the stolen iPads have been stolen from them.

The more he tells me, the more concerned I am.

Give me a hard-to-access tumour with acute haemorrhaging in a seven-year-old and I've usually known how to solve that problem.

But this feels far more complicated.

And far more dangerous.

'Will you help us?' says Wassim, his face so urgent and hopeful I feel a pang just to see it.

'I want to,' I say. 'Very much. I just need to think about how to.'

'Thank you, Felix Salinger,' says Wassim. 'I hope whatever Grandpa Amon gave you at Speerkopf was a very good thing.'

I look at Wassim, caught off guard.

Then I remember it was in Amon's note.

These days I find it hard to talk about things to do with Zelda. But I think Amon would want his grandson to know.

'I was ten when I met your grandpa,' I say. 'The Nazis had just killed my friend, Zelda. She was six. Your grandpa tried to stop them but he couldn't. All he could do was give me something she wanted me to have. A gift she'd got me for my birthday.'

Wassim looks at me, eyes big with sympathy.

'That must have felt like a very special present,' he says.

'It did,' I say quietly. 'From both of them.'

Wassim gives another plate a careful wash.

Then he looks at me again.

'I'm very glad I found the article about you,' he says. 'Thanks for letting the newspaper write it.'

'I'm glad you found it too,' I say.

'And,' says Wassim, 'thank you for looking after yourself so well medically. I'm really glad you're in such good condition.'

I smile.

'You're welcome,' I say.

My phone, on the table, pings as if it agrees.

Wassim turns towards it excitedly, his hands dripping detergent.

'That could be Uncle Otto,' he says.

I go over and peer at the screen.

It is a message, but with no name at the top. Just an international number. I scroll quickly through the long message without reading it, to check the name at the end.

And freeze.

It isn't Otto Kurtz.

It's a name I haven't seen or heard for seventy-three years. A name I've struggled to not even think about.

I stare at it for a long time.

Waiting for the memories to die down.

Memories of the young monster who helped deliver a six-year-old girl into Nazi hands.

And then gloated afterwards about her death.

I'm tempted to fling the phone away.

But I don't.

I owe it to Zelda to handle this, whatever it is.

I scroll back to the beginning of the message and read it.

**Always** keep an open mind, particularly when you want to protect a child in danger.

Try to ignore all feelings of nausea and panic.

A text message won't kill you, even if it was written by a monster.

Dear Doctor Salinger,
We knew each other when we were both very young. I did you great harm, and also great harm to an innocent little girl who was your friend. For those actions, I beg you to accept the apology of an old man who regrets much in his life.

I would have made this apology years ago, but only now do I have the means, thanks to my great-niece who works in the public library where your new friend Wassim Kurtz did his research about you.

I'm also an old man who regrets much of what is happening in the world today. Particularly the suffering of innocent children like Wassim.

I knew Wassim's grandfather before he died.
I know about the people in today's Europe whose
mission is hate. And so I know the problems
young people like Wassim are facing.

I believe I have a solution. I believe you and I,
working together, using our experiences from the
terrible years of our youth, can protect Wassim.
I can't do it alone, and neither can you. But
together, here in Europe, with the locket Wassim's
grandfather gave you at Speerkopf, we can keep
him safe.

I know Eastern Europe is a long journey from
Australia. But please do this for Wassim, Doctor
Salinger. Save him as you have so many other
children. And please allow me to help you protect
him, as my last opportunity to redeem myself in
God's eyes and renounce the evil of my younger
years.

Hopefully and humbly,
Cyryl Szynsky

I stand in my kitchen, staring at the screen,
stunned.

How would Cyryl Szynsky even know my
number? Then I remember that Wassim and Uncle
Otto didn't have any trouble finding my address,
thanks to the mighty power of the internet.

'Felix Salinger,' says Wassim. 'What's the matter?
Is something wrong?'

He's looking at me, concerned.

I realise I must have been staring at the message for a long time. Reading and re-reading. Trying to make sense of it. Trying to digest the crazy notion that somebody like Cyryl Szynsky would want to help a person like Wassim.

'I'm sorry, Wassim,' I say. 'This message isn't from Uncle Otto.'

Wassim's face falls.

I let him have the phone.

My first instinct, after he finishes reading, is to take the phone over to the stove and boil it. Cleanse it of everything to do with Cyryl Szynsky.

But I don't do that.

Wassim is still staring at the screen.

'I know this name,' he says. 'A supermarket near where I live is called Szynsky's. Uncle Otto doesn't like shopping there cause it's Polish and the vodka's too expensive.'

I digest this.

'The Szynskys have been busy,' I mutter. 'When I was a kid, Szynsky's was just one family shop in a small Polish town.'

Even just saying that name is making me feel ill. Let alone thinking of Cyryl Szynsky as the proud owner of a chain of supermarkets scattered across Eastern Europe.

Wassim is frowning.

'The harm that Cyryl Szynsky did to you and your friend,' he says. 'What was it?'

I take a breath and try to calm down a bit.

'I mentioned it a little while ago,' I say quietly.

'Your special friend Zelda?' says Wassim. 'Did Cyryl Szynsky help the Nazis kill her?'

'Sort of,' I say.

Wassim thinks about this.

'And now does he want to help protect me,' says Wassim, 'and probably Uncle Otto as well, to make up for what he did?'

'Looks like it,' I mutter.

Wassim stares at me, uncertain.

'But that's a good thing, isn't it?' he says. 'Good protection, that's what you used to call it when people did it for you in the war.'

I look at his anxious hopeful face and suddenly I feel ashamed.

What am I doing? Why should Wassim miss out on the chance of safety now because of something that happened in 1942?

'Good protection is always good,' I say quietly.

Wassim looks relieved.

'Cyryl Szynsky has got supermarkets,' he says. 'So he must be a very important person, like you. Both of you together could be a really good team. A good protection team.'

I make myself nod.

Wassim's face lights up.

Despite everything, I almost smile to see it.

As long as he's not actually hearing the word no, he's always hopeful.

'Thank you, Felix Salinger,' says Wassim. 'I'm sorry this has brought back bad memories for you. And I'm sorry I ask so many questions. But I do have one more.'

I give him another nod, an encouraging one this time, and he asks it.

'The gift from Zelda that Grandpa Amon gave you,' he says. 'Cyryl Szynsky said it was a locket. He said it'll help keep us safe. How will it?'

I pause for a moment, thinking about the two unexpected gifts that have just come into my life. Zelda's locket and Wassim's hopefulness.

Wassim hands the phone back to me.

'We could ring Cyryl Szynsky and ask him,' he says. 'His number is on the text.'

I look at the phone again.

Wassim is right.

But I'm not ready to ring Cyryl Szynsky yet.

'Before we do that,' I say to Wassim. 'Let's see if we can find out for ourselves.'

**Always** be careful when you dig up a grave.

There's a chance you could dig up things inside yourself as well.

'Is this legal?' says Wassim anxiously.

We're kneeling among the ferns in the little bush cemetery, and Wassim is watching as I gently loosen the soil with my gardening trowel.

'This isn't Zelda's actual grave,' I say. 'It's just a memorial grave we made for her a few years ago. Her locket is here, but her actual bodily remains are in Europe.'

'Whereabouts in Europe?' says Wassim.

I pause, brushing leaves off Zelda's small head-stone. Letting long-ago pain settle a little.

'Good question,' I say. 'I've been asking myself that since 1942. The Nazis murdered millions of people. They often burnt the bodies. Either that, or they threw the bodies into big pits, large numbers at a time, usually in secret locations.'

Wassim doesn't say anything.

I glance at him.

He's busy again, folding his piece of paper.

It's what he did all the way up here in the car. Deep concentration. Carefully folding Uncle Otto's note from the motel into complicated shapes.

I think it was so we wouldn't get on to things he didn't want to talk about.

Things from his past perhaps.

I start scooping the soil out of Zelda's little memorial grave, focusing on doing it gently, but also thinking about something from my past.

Why does Cyryl Szynsky want Zelda's locket?

Is he really offering Wassim good protection?

My heart says, no way. My head says, keep your options open, dopey old man.

The tip of my trowel touches metal in the soil.

'If you're feeling tired,' says Wassim, 'I can do some digging.'

'Thanks,' I say. 'But here it is.'

My shaky hands take a few moments to get the lid off the small lacquered metal box. Then, by its slender chain, I lift the locket out.

Wassim leans forward and peers at it.

'It's got hinges,' he says. 'Does it open?'

I brush off a few wisps of ageing cotton wool, open the small metal heart and hand it to him.

Wassim takes the locket and studies it.

He taps it and shakes it and blows some dust out of it. Then peers at it even more closely.

'What's this scratched on the inside?' he says.

'Little pictures,' I say. 'See?'

'Yes,' says Wassim. 'What are they?'

'Stick figures,' I say. 'Of Zelda and me. With some dancing chickens. Zelda must have done this after she bought the locket. To make it an even more special birthday present.'

Wassim frowns.

He spits into the locket, rubs it on his coat, and peers at it again.

'Do you think she had any help?' he says.

'She probably wouldn't have needed it,' I say. 'She was very good at chickens.'

I resist the temptation to add that Zelda would also have been very good at telling off people who spit on other people's most precious possessions.

Wassim is staring at the locket, puzzled.

'Some of these chickens are different,' he says. 'They're not the same as the one holding Zelda's hand.'

I squint at the other three chickens.

'They're not drawn so well,' says Wassim. 'And the scratch marks are kind of deeper.'

I clean my glasses, then angle the locket so the morning sun shines more directly on to it.

Wassim is right.

This is strange.

The other three chickens are drawn in a different style. And whoever drew them has scratched much harder.

I've had a precious locket for seventy-seven years, and I've never noticed this before.

Probably because all I've seen is sad memories. Zelda looking at me with a loving frown, saying, 'Don't you know anything?'

Which, when it came to this locket, I didn't.

'Thank you, Wassim,' I say. 'It's not just Zelda who's good at chickens.'

Wassim doesn't reply.

He's still peering into the locket.

I wonder if he's asking the same question I am. Did somebody else scratch those extra chickens? And if they did, why?

'I wish this locket was bigger and easier to see,' says Wassim.

'I've got a magnifying glass in the glove box of the car,' I say. 'That'll give us a better look at it.'

Wassim helps me to my feet.

I wince as my legs straighten out and the blood flows through them again.

I can see Wassim wants to hurry ahead.

'I'll catch you up,' I say. 'Don't forget Jumble is in the car, guarding it. Try not to wake him up.'

Wassim grins and hurries off.

After a couple of steps he stops, turns back and pulls something from his coat pocket.

'This is for you,' he says, handing it to me.

It's Uncle Otto's note, carefully folded origami-style into an elegant shape, long and slender with tucked-back wings.

'What a beautiful bird,' I say.

'It's a stork,' says Wassim. 'For good luck. It's to say thank you for helping me and Uncle Otto.'

He smiles at me for a moment, then sprints away along the bush path towards the carpark.

'Thank you, Wassim,' I call after him.

I don't think he hears me over the sigh of the breeze in the leaves.

But I also don't think he did this to be thanked.

Which touches me even more.

I put the bird carefully into my pocket.

Then I pick up my walking stick and set off down the path, my head full of questions about Cyryl Szynsky and Amon Kurtz and the locket.

Along with a hope that whatever the answers turn out to be, they'll include good protection for a brave and lonely boy.

I walk with this fond hope until I do hear something over the sigh of the breeze in the leaves.

Wassim screaming.

**Always** unmistakable, death.

Even when you're in shock, you know it as soon as you see it.

I burst out of the trees, my legs all over the place, and see him on the ground, not moving, his throat red and wet, and I know.

Oh.

Oh, Jumble.

Wassim is on his knees next to Jumble, sobbing.

The car door is open.

Nobody inside. Nobody near. Nobody anywhere in the carpark. No other cars.

Just my car.

With something smeared on the rear door.

A symbol.

Wet and red.

I recognise it. An ancient noble symbol. Stolen by people who aren't noble at all. Trying to use history to flatter their rancid ideas.

I turn my back on it.

Hurry over to Jumble and Wassim.

Kneel down and gently put my hand on Wassim's arm. Check Jumble's pulse with the other. Because even when you know, you still hope.

Nothing.

'Felix,' sobs Wassim. 'It's the Weasels' symbol. How did they get here? Why did they do this?'

I shake my head.

I don't know.

'Uncle Otto said the Weasels might want to hurt me,' sobs Wassim. 'He didn't say anything about an innocent dog.'

I stare at Wassim, taking this in.

'Did they see you just now?' I say.

Wassim shakes his head.

'I was still on the bush track,' he says. 'I heard a car driving away. By the time I got here, it was gone. There was just Jumble.'

Wassim closes his eyes. I put my arm round his shoulders. After a while I lean forward and gently lay my hanky over Jumble's blank eyes.

I made Jumble stay in the car just now, in case he decided to do some grave-digging of his own. The look he gave me. Even when I promised him it wouldn't be for long.

I'm sorry, I say silently to him.

Now I have to close my eyes.

But only for a moment. Because Wassim asks an important question.

'How did they know where to find us?' he says.

It's a very good question.

I didn't see a vehicle following us.

I wasn't looking for one, but partisan training stays with you even when you're old and dopey. You notice those things without looking, unless you've forgotten your glasses.

So if the Weasels didn't follow us, how did they know where we are?

My phone starts ringing in the car.

I stumble over and grab it from the glove box.

No number on the screen.

'Hello?' I say.

'Is that Doctor Felix Salinger?' says a woman's voice in Polish.

'Yes,' I say.

Please, not now, I beg silently. Not another kind ex-patient ringing to invite me to a son or daughter's school graduation.

'Text message arriving,' says the woman. 'To be acknowledged when you've read it.'

She hangs up.

I stare at the screen, puzzled. Definitely not a patient. And I've never heard of a phone company offering this service.

A text pings on to the screen.

Be on guard. They know where to find you, the people who hate. They've done library research too. Europe is safer. Don't delay. Cyryl

There's a return number. I check, and it's the same as the number on Cyryl Szynsky's other message.

I ring it.

No answer.

I send a text.

Message seen. We need to talk.

I switch the phone off and turn to hurry back to Wassim. But he's standing close, staring at me, his face wet with misery.

'Uncle Otto's war must have started,' he says. 'And now the Weasels think you're their enemy too. Which is my fault.'

I try to speak.

I need a few moments before I can.

Partly because of Jumble, but also because of this boy whose hopeful heart is becoming a casualty too.

'Wassim,' I say. 'None of this is your fault.'

'It is,' says Wassim. 'Bad people can track phones. I've seen it in movies. It's how the Weasels found us. You're here with your phone. Because of me. So it's my fault Jumble's dead.'

I take hold of Wassim's shoulders.

'If we're going to get through all this,' I say softly, 'there's an important thing you have to remember. People like the Weasels want us to blame ourselves for things they do. Because it makes them stronger and us weaker. But you're not weak, Wassim. You're brave and determined and clever. And the Weasels are scared of that.'

I grab a cloth and wipe the symbol off my car.

Wassim watches me.

I can see he's thinking about what I just said to him. He doesn't look totally convinced.

But he nods bravely.

He also bravely digs Jumble's grave.

He doesn't have to. But he insists.

And he suggests doing it next to Zelda's grave.

The perfect place.

It's hard work. My gardening trowel is a tenth the size of a proper shovel and Jumble isn't a little dog, so digging that hole must be exhausting.

Wassim won't let me help.

'I want it to be my job,' he says, panting with the effort. 'Your job can be looking after the locket.'

After a few minutes he pauses and looks at me, as if he just thought of something.

'Did you get Jumble's name from the dog in the Richmal Crompton books?' he says.

'Yes,' I say. 'All through my childhood I hoped that one day I'd have a dog called Jumble.'

'I'm glad you did,' says Wassim.

He goes back to digging, kneeling and bending forward into the hole as he digs it deeper.

Watching him, I remember another grave being dug a long time ago.

A grave for another innocent dog.

We buried Leopold under a big tree on Genia's farm. Me and Zelda, weeping and digging.

Zelda muttering angrily about the Nazis who'd killed him, and the young thug who'd distracted us with bullying so we couldn't warn our loyal friend.

'I want to slap those Nazis,' said Zelda. 'And Cyryl Szynsky.'

I agreed.

And then, while we carried on digging, I pushed Cyryl Szynsky out of my mind.

I didn't want that monster lurking in my thoughts anywhere near Zelda, or Genia, or dear brave Leopold.

But now he's back in my mind, I can remember something else. The day everyone in the local town was made to line up in the street and watch Nazi troops marching past.

Zelda poking her tongue out.

Cyryl Szynsky giggling. And being grabbed by angry Nazis and slapped and punched until he was on the ground, sobbing at the cruel injustice of the world and the sight of his own blood.

Because he was just a kid.

Like us.

'Nearly finished, Felix,' calls Wassim.

I blink and remember where I am.

Wassim is crouching in the hole now, almost out of sight as he digs. He's neatly stacked the piles of earth around the edges, making sure it doesn't spill on to Zelda's grave.

'Good work,' I say to Wassim. 'You're doing a wonderful job.'

Wassim says something that sounds like thanks, but he says it in another language.

I look at him, amazed.

'Wassim,' I say. 'How many languages do you speak?'

'Just three,' pants Wassim. 'The one I speak at school, the one I speak at home with Uncle Otto, and the one Mum and Dad taught me. Dad lived in England before he met Mum.'

Wassim carries on digging.

I go back to watching him. This boy who has so much to give, and who I suspect has had so much taken from him.

He turns to me again.

'Do you think Zelda will mind,' he says. 'Having a dog buried next to her memorial grave?'

I shake my head. Wassim looks relieved.

'I don't think she will either,' he says. 'I think they'll be good friends.'

I smile.

'I think they will too,' I say.

A few more minutes of digging, and I manage to persuade Wassim the hole is deep enough.

We scatter a bed of leaves into the bottom of it, wrap Jumble carefully in his car blanket, and then together we slowly lower him down.

Then we stand side by side and say our goodbyes to him.

'Thank you, old friend,' I whisper.

'Thank you, new friend,' whispers Wassim.

Gently, together, we cover him with earth.

A few more tearful words.

Then I quietly tell Zelda that I hope she enjoys her new neighbour, and I turn to Wassim to suggest that we go back to the car.

Wassim is standing still and silent at the edge of Jumble's grave, head bowed.

I wait.

He looks up and sees me.

'Sorry, Felix,' he says. 'Do you mind if I have a little bit more time?'

'Of course not,' I say.

'It's partly for Jumble,' he says, 'and partly for Mum and Dad. I wasn't allowed to go to their funeral.'

He bows his head again.

I look at him standing there, his thin shoulders sheltering himself and his memories, and I make a silent promise.

I'm still alive, Wassim, because a long time ago people gave me good protection, even if it cost them everything.

Now I'm going to do the same for you.

# Wassim

**Always** seek justice.

That was Mum's motto.

She did it whenever she could, including when the laundromat mangled her undies.

I tell Felix about it as we drive back to his place. And then I tell him how much I want to get justice for Jumble.

But there's something I don't tell him.

How, to give him time to recover from Jumble dying, I've decided to get the justice on my own.

'Cyryl Szynsky will help,' is all I say.

'I hope he does,' says Felix. 'He could probably help a lot if he wants to. His family doesn't just own supermarkets. His uncle was a government minister. His father was a mayor. I'm guessing the Szynsky family know a lot of powerful people.'

I wait for Felix to say more.

He doesn't. He's been very quiet and thoughtful since we left the cemetery.

I know how he feels.

I didn't want to chat for weeks after Mum and Dad died. That's why I've decided not to tell Felix about the rest of my plan until later, when he's feeling more up to it.

It's a good plan, but I'm sad I'll have to say goodbye to Felix for a while. Still, he can have some quiet time on his own, which is important when a family member dies.

Plus he'll also have time to find another dog to love, and he won't have to worry about it being in danger from the Weasels.

Because me and Cyryl Szynsky are going to take care of that.

I'll ask Felix to lend me the locket and then I'll ask his friend at the airport to help me catch a plane home with the ticket I've got.

When I arrive, I'll meet Cyryl Szynsky at his supermarket. And tell him he can see the locket, and hold it, and even take photos of it, but only if he gets good protection for Uncle Otto and justice for Jumble, including big punishments for the Weasels.

I think I can do that on my own.

I hope I can.

'Wassim,' says Felix. 'Here's what we'll do now. I'll grab some things from home. Then we'll go to a friend's place, which is quiet and tucked away, so we can make contact with Cyryl Szynsky without being interrupted by unwelcome visitors.'

I nod enthusiastically, so he can see I agree.

'I bet you've got loads of friends,' I say.

Felix gives me a look.

Sort of amused and sad at the same time.

'I used to,' he says. 'But most of my friends have turned into library books.'

I look at Felix, puzzled.

'Checked out,' he says quietly. 'And most of the ones still here, poor loves, have a bit of a struggle recognising me.'

I don't know what to say.

I haven't got many friends either, but at least I'm young and there's hope for the future.

Felix suddenly looks cheerful.

'But,' he says, 'I do have lovely ex-patients. One in particular who is a dear friend as well. And her place is very tucked away.'

'I think hiding there is a good plan,' I say.

It is. And it'll fit in perfectly with mine.

Specially if me and Uncle Otto can get back from Europe in time to help Felix choose his new dog.

While Felix drives, I study the locket.

I'm hoping Felix's magnifying glass will help me find information I can swap with Cyryl Szynsky for justice.

It should do. Felix says it's good at finding bad ingredients on food labels in the supermarket.

And it does show very definitely that three of the four dancing chickens are different.

Deeper scratches and a different way of drawing.

Which is a puzzle.

If Zelda did those chickens too, why did she change her chicken style?

Felix told me she bought the locket only half an hour before she was killed, so she wouldn't have had time for an art lesson.

But if somebody else did them, why?

I stare at the chickens. And notice something.

The second chicken from the right, the one doing crazy dancing like it's had too much vodka, has got a weird beak.

The beak looks more like a nose. Or a feather gone curly. Or a number six.

I blink and stare harder.

It is a six.

And I see something else. Both the chicken's legs look like sevens. And one of its feet is like a three.

'Felix,' I yell. 'Look.'

He can't because he's driving. But as soon as he's recovered from the shock of me yelling, he pulls over to the side of the road.

I show him the beak and the legs and the foot.

The six and the sevens and the three.

'You're right,' says Felix, looking a bit stunned.

We examine the other chickens. Their wings, beaks, feet, feathers, thighs and the wobbly bits on their heads and under their chins.

More numbers.

And sometimes letters.

'The chickens are built of numbers and letters,' I say, my voice squeaky with amazement. 'You've been sent secret information by chicken.'

Felix is looking amazed too.

He's probably wondering how he missed seeing all this. Which he shouldn't feel bad about, not somebody as busy as he's been.

'It must have been Grandpa Amon,' I say. 'You told me how he found the locket in Zelda's coat. Nobody else would have had a chance to do any extra scratching.'

Felix nods.

'Well done, Wassim,' he says. 'When I said how you were very good at chickens, I should have said extremely good.'

We grin at each other.

Felix reaches into the glove box and hands me a pen and a parking ticket.

'While I drive,' he says, 'can you make a list of all the numbers and letters? Then we can try to work out what the information is in Grandpa Amon's secret message.'

As we turn the corner into Felix's street, I feel a bit disappointed.

I've made a list of chicken numbers and letters like Felix asked me, and I was hoping to find at least a couple of clues for him.

But I haven't spotted a single one.

I confess this to Felix.

He's very understanding.

'Same with crosswords,' he says. 'Takes hours to get a single clue sometimes. The trick is to expect the unexpec–'

Felix doesn't finish the word.

He stares out of the car, frowning.

I see why. Everything around the car has gone hazy. And there's the smell of smoke.

'What's going on?' says Felix.

I don't know. It smells a bit like tyre smoke, but you'd need about a hundred screeching cars to make this much.

Felix has slowed right down, steering the car through the haze, and suddenly we see it.

Water and soot on the road.

Fire trucks blocking the street.

People out of their houses, looking shocked, some of them seeing Felix's car and nudging each other.

Felix suddenly pulls over as we get near to his place, our wheels bumping up on to the kerb.

I stare out the window, horrified.

Felix is staring too, looking dazed and hurt and shocked, like someone's just hit him.

We don't say anything.

We don't need to.

We both know who did this.

**Always** breathe slowly through your nose when you're having shock and unhappiness.

Specially when there's smoke blowing around and you don't want to breathe in the sooty black bits of your poor friend's home.

I help Felix out of the car and we go over to look at the awful sight. The burnt crumpled mess that used to be Felix's house.

For a few moments Felix just stares at it.

Then he tells one of the firefighters who he is.

She puts her arm round him.

'So sorry, love,' she says.

I don't understand anything she says after that. She's got a very strong Australian accent and a lot of it doesn't get through her firefighter's mask.

'Thank you, Tommo,' says another firefighter, a man with a weary voice and important-looking badges on his overalls.

I'm not sure what 'Tommo' means exactly.

But the other firefighter gets the message. She gives Felix and me a sympathetic look and goes to help the other firefighters straighten out a hose.

Watching her go, I spot something.

Felix's mailbox, near the kerb. With something poking out of it. A piece of paper.

Not in an envelope like you'd normally expect.

The older firefighter, who must be an officer, asks Felix a couple of questions, nodding towards the wreckage. The only words I understand through his mask are *people* and *animals*.

Felix shakes his head.

'Nobody was left in the house,' he says.

The officer looks relieved.

'Lucky,' he says.

I don't say anything. I don't tell the officer that Felix's luck ended the second I banged on his door this morning.

Instead I go over to the mailbox and pull out the piece of paper.

It's scorched and yellow from the heat of the fire, but I can still make out what's drawn on it in black marker pen.

The Weasels symbol.

I take the piece of paper over to the Felix, who's still talking to the officer.

Felix looks at the symbol. He hands the paper to the officer and explains what it is. The officer peers at it, shrugs, says something I can't make out, and takes it over to the fire truck.

'He thinks it's just local kids mucking around,' says Felix to me quietly. 'Leave it for now.'

I don't want to leave it for now. I want to grab the officer by his badges and give him a shake.

But then I remember that a fire officer would probably have to report that to the police, so I make myself calm down.

Felix is telling the officer about something in the house. Something important.

'I need you to find it if you can,' he says. 'Please.'

The officer frowns doubtfully.

Felix gives him a look. A pleading look, but stern as well. It's probably the same look Felix would have given in an operating theatre if the person doing the anaesthetic wanted to go and play golf before the operation was finished.

The officer goes across to the other firefighters and starts talking to them.

Felix is amazing.

Staying hopeful that anything could survive in these smoking ruins. When it's the second time this has happened to him. With his last house it was a bushfire, but still.

How much stress like this can a person with a very ancient heart and Nazi-damaged knees take?

I try to say something to help Felix feel better. About how belongings can always be replaced. Specially if you know a good second-hand shop.

But nothing comes out of my mouth except unhappy sounds.

Felix gives my arm a squeeze.

I give his arm a squeeze back, which I wouldn't normally do to an adult, but I think it's OK when somebody's just lost their whole house for the second time, and their whole dog.

'You weren't exaggerating,' says Felix. 'About our friends the Weasels.'

We think our gloomy thoughts for a while.

'Felix,' I say, 'do you think they're trying to scare us? Make us hide under a rock, so we can't help Uncle Otto with his war.'

'Could be,' says Felix.

He goes back to his thoughts.

I do the same, and decide two things.

One is that the Weasels will never scare me away from saving Uncle Otto and getting justice.

The other thing I decide is that I can't leave Felix here in Australia.

I can't bear the idea of him hiding under a rock, or even under a friend's house, having sad thoughts about how he lost his dog and his home. That kind of stress does more than hurt old knees or an old heart. It can stop a person ever being happy again.

Felix's phone pings. He stares at the screen.

'Look at this,' he says.

It's another text message.

Serious danger in Australia. Get out now. Tickets at airport. Bring boy and locket. Cyril

Felix and I look at each other.

94

'If he's paid for our plane tickets,' I say, 'he must really want to be a good protection team with you.'

Which is very good.

Somebody calls Felix's name.

The firefighting officer is back.

He's with two of the other firefighters, who are dragging something towards us. Something black and heavy and covered with wet ash.

A small metal safe.

I feel the heat coming from it.

One of the firefighters drags a hose over and starts spraying it.

I hope it's fireproof. And waterproof. Because suddenly I'm hopeful about what's in there.

Felix puts on some big leather gloves that one of the firefighters gives him.

He crouches down and starts clicking the dial on the front of the safe. Moving it round to one number, then another, then another.

The firefighters must think they shouldn't see, because they look away.

More secret numbers.

Suddenly I have another thought.

One that makes my insides start revving, that's how much I want it to be true.

A thought about why the Weasels put so much effort into trying to make us hide under a rock. Why they took a dog's life and destroyed a house and wrecked all the washing in a whole street.

The Weasels are scared of the chicken numbers.

They don't want us to show them to Uncle Otto or to Cyryl Szynsky, because those numbers could help us win the war against them.

We just have to find out how.

Felix stops clicking the dial and the door of the safe swings open.

I hold my breath.

Felix takes out a bundle of papers.

Yes.

Lying on top of the bundle is a passport.

I'm very relieved to see it. If Felix's passport had burnt to bits, we couldn't do my new plan.

Take the locket to Poland.

Me and Felix.

Crack the code and share its secrets.

So that Uncle Otto and Cyryl Szynsky and me and Felix can work together to defeat the Weasels forever.

**Always** expect the unexpected, that's one of Felix's mottos.

This is definitely unexpected.

We're driving into an underground carpark in the middle of Melbourne's city centre when we're meant to be on our way to Felix's friend's quiet and tucked-away house.

Is the house here in the city centre?

That isn't very tucked away.

'Felix,' I say after he's parked the car. 'Why are we here?'

Felix looks at me and takes a deep breath.

'Wassim,' he says. 'I know you don't want this. But I have to at least try. I promise I'll be careful and cautious.'

I look at Felix.

I haven't got a clue what he's talking about.

'And,' says Felix, 'I won't go ahead if I see there's any chance of what you fear happening.'

I stare at Felix.

I'm starting to feel very stressed.

Because suddenly I think I do know what he's talking about.

'The slightest chance at all,' says Felix, 'of Uncle Otto being put in more danger by the police.'

Felix has been gone twenty minutes now.

I hope he comes back soon, because I want to say sorry for swearing at him. Plus I don't think my trust can last much longer.

I know that Felix will be super-careful with the police. I trust him about that. He's left me here in the car so I can't be dragged off to a child welfare home for my own good. That's an example of how careful he's being.

And he's brave to even go into the police headquarters, when they haven't even said he has to.

But I just don't know how he's going to manage things in there.

How can he tell the police about the danger Uncle Otto's in without mentioning Uncle Otto?

I take a deep breath.

I tell myself that eminent surgeons are good at choosing their words carefully. For example, when they have to tell a desperate family that a poor patient has died.

I wish I hadn't thought of that example.

I take another deep breath.

I'm going to try and last another five minutes.

Felix has suffered a lot today, and most of it is my fault, and now he's just trying to keep me and Uncle Otto safe, so if my trust runs out, maybe my gratefulness will help me hang on.

When Felix comes back, I'm still hanging on.

'No good, I'm afraid,' he says after he gets into the car.

'What happened?' I say anxiously. 'What did the police say to you?'

'Not much, really,' says Felix. 'But I saw what they were thinking. That because I could only tell them part of what's going on, I'm going dotty.'

I give Felix a sympathetic look.

'So the police won't help us?' I say.

'I asked them to put me in touch with Interpol in Europe,' says Felix. 'Who would definitely not be involved with the Weasels. There was muttering about me watching too many spy movies. Then the police said they couldn't promise anything, plus the paperwork could take several weeks.'

I don't bother saying that's several weeks too long when a war's already started.

Felix knows it is.

'So it's just us,' says Felix. 'And Uncle Otto and maybe Cyryl Szynsky. Are you OK with that?'

I nod.

Felix sighs.

'Wassim,' he says. 'I'm really sorry for putting you through this police stuff.'

'I understand why you had to,' I say. 'Sometimes grown-ups have to do things they don't want to do.'

Felix nods and smiles.

'Thanks for understanding,' he says.

He starts the engine.

'And thank you,' he says, 'for being so kind and gentle.'

I give him a puzzled look.

He smiles at me again.

'Only swearing at me in your third language,' he says. 'The one I don't understand.'

**Always** be nice to a very old friend of your new friend. Specially when she's one of the few old friends Felix has got left.

It's a good motto and I'm hoping I can live up to it. But now we're nearly arriving at Ruby's house, I'm not sure.

What if she wrecks all our plans and stops me and Felix going back to Europe to get justice for Jumble and revenge for Felix's house and victory for Uncle Otto?

I'm not saying she will. But Felix has told me a lot about Ruby and I'm worried.

I've known Felix in person for about five and a half hours. Ruby has known him for seventy-three years, ever since Felix was fourteen and he helped her be born medically.

So she might be bossy about protecting him from danger because she might have forgotten how brave Felix still is.

She already knows about the Weasels. Felix told her about them on the phone in the car.

Oh well. She might be able to stop Felix going, and that would be tragic.

But she can't stop me because I'm a European citizen and I've got a passport to prove it.

Here goes.

We pull up in Ruby's driveway and I try to stop my worry cylinders from blowing a gasket.

'I think you'll like her,' says Felix.

'Mmmm,' I say.

We get out of the car.

The front door of the house opens. A woman in a very colourful dress steps out.

I hold my breath and wait to see if she flicks her long curly grey hair out of her eyes, gives Felix a stern look, and says, 'Europe? Tomorrow? With a kid you've only just met? Are you crazy?'

She doesn't.

'Hello, Ruby,' says Felix.

Ruby comes towards us, having tears.

She hugs Felix, hugs me who she's never even met, says some very loving things about Jumble, some very sympathetic things about Felix's house, then starts behaving like a very experienced, super-organised chief financial officer of one of Australia's biggest charities.

Which she was before she retired.

'Flights are all sorted,' she says as she leads us

into the house. 'Hotel, ditto. Wassim, do you like chocolate biscuits? I've got very delicious ones with strawberry caramel in them.'

I'm feeling a bit dazed, so I just nod.

Ruby takes us into the kitchen and introduces me to her partner, Claire, who gives me a hug too.

Felix hugs Claire, gives her his car key, and she goes out the back door.

'We'll hide Felix's car in our garage,' Ruby says to me. 'We'll take you to the airport in our car.'

I don't know what to say.

They only met me two minutes ago and they're already offering good protection.

'Thank you,' I say.

'Sit,' says Ruby to me with a smile. 'Drink. Eat.'

Felix is smiling too as we all sit at the kitchen table. Ruby pours cups of tea and slides a big plate of chocolate biscuits towards me.

And then looks at me, concerned.

'You must be boiling,' she says. 'Let me take your hat and scarf.'

'No thanks,' I say, trying not to panic. 'I'm fine, really, thank you.'

One glimpse of my neck, and they'd probably decide I'm too bruised to go on the mission.

'It's OK,' says Felix to Ruby. 'Wassim's getting ready to go back to the cold weather.'

Ruby smiles at me.

'Sorry, Wassim,' she says. 'Didn't think of that. Please, have a biscuit.'

I take one and eat it.

Ruby's right, it is delicious. The people she gave charity to at her job must have been delighted if they got these as well.

'First things first,' says Ruby. 'Sheree Nile has confirmed that Uncle Otto departed this morning on his booked flight.'

Felix gives me a concerned glance.

I give him a look back, to show him I was pretty sure Uncle Otto had gone.

Ruby puts her hand on my arm.

'Sheree knows people in lots of the airlines, Wassim,' she says. 'She helped me fix up Felix's ticket so you're both on a new flight to your local airport. A booking nobody else knows about, so you won't have any bad guys greeting you at the other end. Also, as you're not flying back with the adult you arrived with, I asked her to fix up the paperwork to get you on board.'

I stare at Ruby, amazed.

I almost wish I was staying in Australia longer, so she could teach me how to be a chief financial officer. But now I know for sure that Uncle Otto's gone back, I must too.

Felix is looking at Ruby as well, and I can see how grateful he is.

'Thank you,' he says. 'I hope one day I can . . .'

Ruby puts her finger over his lips.

'You already repaid me,' she says to him quietly. 'Seventy-three years ago.'

They look at each other in a way that makes me feel emotional. It's amazing to see them having so much fondness for each other about something that happened nearly a hundred years ago.

'So,' says Ruby, 'no luck getting through?'

'Not yet,' says Felix. 'I rang Cyryl Szynsky from the car, but it was after midnight over there. I left him a message saying we were on our way.'

Ruby nods.

'I'm glad you're finally going back, Felix,' she says. 'OK, you've left it a bit late. Seventy-three years between visits. And a Glories of Eastern Europe bus tour would have been safer . . .'

Felix smiles.

Ruby doesn't. She puts her hand on his arm.

'Please, Felix,' she says. 'Be careful. You've seen how those Iron Weasels operate. No anaesthetic.'

Felix is looking serious now too.

'I know,' he says quietly. 'Thank you.'

Ruby gets up, goes to a kitchen drawer, comes back and puts something on the table with a clunk.

A gun.

She sees me staring at it.

'My mother left it to me in her will,' she says. 'Well, in her underwear drawer, actually.'

Felix has told me about Ruby's mum, Anya.

She was a teenager when he met her in the war, with wild hair like Ruby's, and a pink coat, and a loaded gun she loved jamming into the mouths of people who deserved a fright.

This gun probably.

But I'm confused.

A person like Ruby would know about airport security, and how you can't lend a gun to a friend who's going on a plane.

Plus it's not even necessary. Uncle Otto has a gun hidden behind the vegetables under the sink.

Before I can tell Ruby that, she sits down next to me and puts her hand gently on my arm.

'If a trip to Weasel territory is feeling too scary, Wassim,' she says, 'you're very welcome to stay with us till Felix gets back with Uncle Otto. It's a very comfortable place to hide. You've tasted the biscuits. And I can promise you good protection.'

She nods towards the gun.

I don't know what to say. It's very kind of her, but didn't Felix explain to her that we're a team?

'Thanks, Ruby,' says Felix gently. 'That's a very generous offer. But I think you can see how Wassim is feeling. Australia is a very long way from home when someone you love is in danger.'

Felix has summed it up perfectly.

But I don't want Ruby to think I'm ungrateful.

'When Felix was ten,' I say to her, 'the man who was being his father was taken away by some Polish police who were friends with the Nazis. Felix had a good place to hide too, but he didn't stay there, he went to help Gabriek.'

Ruby nods. I think she understands.

She gives me a hug.

'Be safe,' she whispers.

'Thank you,' I say.

Ruby puts her hand on Felix's cheek.

'This is a wonderful, what you're doing,' she says softly to him. 'However it turns out. I wish when you were ten, you'd had someone like you.'

'I did,' says Felix quietly. 'Several of them. And for me they made sure it did work out.'

I know who he means. I've read about them. The people who gave him good protection.

I think about Uncle Otto's gun again.

Well, Felix, I say silently, you've got me now. And I'm going to give you very good protection.

**Always** be as practical as you can.

That was one of Dad's mottos.

Most of the people on this plane are not being practical at all. Just lazing about watching movies and reading magazines and eating peanuts out of very small packets.

Not me and Felix.

We've got our tray tables down and we're being very practical with the numbers and letters from the locket. Trying to work out what Grandpa Amon and the chickens are telling us.

One of the chickens is made up of just letters, so we're concentrating on that one first. Trying to see what words the letters make.

I've copied the letters on to a big piece of paper so we can both look at them.

Z H T S A C

It's OK, nobody else can see them. Not even other passengers with strong glasses.

We've got three seats, thanks to Sheree.

I've got the one by the window, Felix is in the seat next to me, and the one on the other side of him next to the aisle is empty.

So nobody can peek.

Felix gives a frustrated groan, a quiet one.

I see why.

He's just written another word on the piece of paper. Another English one. Which can't possibly be part of a secret message from Grandpa Amon, because Grandpa Amon didn't speak English.

Felix looks at our list of words and sighs.

*CAT*
*SAT*
*HAT*
*CHAT*
*CAST*
*CASH*

All English. If we're going to crack this code, we need words in Polish, which is what Grandpa Amon spoke. We've been searching for some since we took off from Melbourne, and so far we haven't found a single one.

'Oh well,' I say to Felix, trying to keep his spirits up. 'It could be worse. At least we've got another twenty-eight hours.'

I must have started to nod off, because when Felix whispers something a bit loudly, I open my eyes and for a sec I don't know where I am.

Then I see the flight map on the screen in front of me, which shows that we're ten thousand metres above the world.

'German,' says Felix.

I look at him, confused.

'Amon worked with Nazi soldiers,' says Felix. 'He told me once how he translated for Nazi officers when they were having drinks with Polish women. So he must have spoken at least some German.'

Felix writes a new word on his piece of paper, his hands shaking even more than they usually do.

*SCHATZ*

Which is amazing.

It uses all the letters from the chicken.

'What does it mean?' I say.

'It's a German word for something that could explain a lot about what's been going on,' says Felix. '*Schatz* means treasure.'

I stare at Felix. I stare at the word on the piece of paper. I stare at Felix again.

I'm on all eight cylinders.

This is incredible.

Is treasure what Grandpa Amon wanted to tell Felix about?

'Yes,' I say. 'Of course. The Nazis had treasure, I've read about it. Treasure they stole from other people and kept for themselves.'

Felix nods.

But I don't think he's really listening.

He's staring at the word on the piece of paper.

Not excited like me, more sort of dazed and emotional.

I don't blame him.

Treasure could help him pay his dear friend Ruby back for the clothes and shoes and pills she wouldn't let him pay for at the airport.

'Felix,' I say.

I wait till he looks at me.

'Do you think Cyryl Szynsky would know about Nazi treasure?' I say.

Felix thinks about this.

'Yes,' he says. 'Almost certainly. There's a story about Nazi treasure that's often in the media. A Nazi treasure train, lost somewhere in Eastern Europe during the war. Hidden for seventy years and waiting to be discovered.'

'A train?' I say excitedly.

That was too loud. I lower my voice. The plane engines are loud too, but this plane is crowded and I don't want to take chances.

Not with treasure.

And not with what's just burst into my mind.

'Felix,' I say. 'Uncle Otto told me once about my great-grandfather, who was Grandpa Amon's father. He was German. He worked for the Nazis. As a train driver.'

Felix stares at me.

He doesn't look dazed any more. He looks like his brain is on eight cylinders too, and he's thinking the same thing as me.

'If Amon's father was involved in the transport of Nazi treasure,' say Felix, 'Amon would probably have known.'

'And,' I say, trying to keep my voice quiet and not too squeaky with excitement, 'if he wanted to say sorry to you for not saving Zelda, what better thing than treasure?'

My mind is going on nine cylinders.

'The chicken numbers,' I say to Felix. 'I bet the numbers will tell us where the treasure is.'

'You could be right,' says Felix.

Thoughts crowd into my head.

'We'll need a big truck to transport the treasure,' I say. 'And we'll need some tools. The train doors will probably all be locked. The Nazis wouldn't leave treasure in an unlocked train. Uncle Otto will know where we can get breaking-in tools.'

Felix does a little laugh that sounds a bit painful.

'What's wrong?' I say.

'I've just remembered something that got burnt in my bushfire house,' says Felix. 'Something that would have been very useful. My friend Gabriek gave them to me when I was twelve.'

Of course. I read about it in the article.

'Lock-picking tools,' I say. 'For picking locks.'

Felix smiles sadly and nods.

I have an idea.

I don't say anything now because I don't know if it'll work, but when we get to where we're going, I'll see if it will.

'Anyway,' says Felix. 'We've got to find the train first.'

He's right. Back to work.

Make those numbers tell us where the train is.

But before we do, I can't resist thinking about what it'll be like when we find the treasure.

Sometimes, when I was little, Mum used to get upset with her work.

*I hate people with lots of money,* she used to yell, waving her arms. *They think they can do anything they want.*

She was an accountant, so she knew what she was talking about.

So look out, Weasels, when we find the treasure, we'll be able to do anything we want, including to you.

**Always** be patient.

Ms Molinowski is a big believer in that.

She says swearing at things never makes them easier to understand. Not maps, not instruction manuals, and definitely not teachers.

Or numbers.

Numbers at school are even harder than letters, and it's turning out they're just as hard in secret messages about treasure.

I've been sitting in this plane seat staring at the chicken numbers for hours.

I even copied them on to a big piece of paper because that worked with the letters.

It hasn't with the numbers.

Felix and I have tried everything we can think of to find out what they mean. To see if they can help us find the lost Nazi treasure train.

Nothing.

Poor Felix is worn out.

He's having a nap in his seat, snoring quietly.

I'm young, so I'm still awake, struggling to find the answer.

'No!' yells Felix, and wakes up suddenly.

People in the seats near us all look, which isn't good right in the middle of a highly top-secret data-processing operation.

Felix is looking around too, blinking, as if he's not sure where he is.

'Are you OK?' I whisper. 'You shouted.'

Felix glances anxiously at the people around us, who luckily have lost interest.

'Sorry,' he says. 'I was having a bad dream.'

Poor Felix.

It was probably a scary dream. About our war against the Weasels. When I told Felix about the treasure helping us win the war, he looked a bit uncertain and doubtful.

Now Felix is looking more sad than anything.

He's staring at the German word on the piece of paper.

'I was dreaming about Zelda,' he says quietly. 'And about something I haven't mentioned to you. How the word *Schatz* has a second meaning. It's an old-fashioned meaning, but it wasn't when Amon was young. As well as treasure, *Schatz* also means precious person.'

I didn't know that.

No wonder Felix has been feeling so emotional.

Grandpa Amon's secret word must have made Felix remember things that are even more precious to him than gold and diamonds.

All the people he's lost in his life.

'I'm sorry, Wassim,' says Felix. 'I know I should be helping you with the numbers, but I just need to close my eyes for a bit longer.'

'That's OK,' I say. 'I understand. I hope you have a good dream this time. About you and Zelda when you were happy.'

'Thank you,' says Felix, patting my arm.

He takes his glasses off and closes his eyes.

I stare at the numbers.

My job is even more important now.

Ms Malinowski says we must be methodical and check our work. So everything me and Felix tried with the numbers before, I try again.

I turn the numbers into letters.

1=A, 2=B, 3=C, and so on.

I use the letters to try and make a useful sentence.

An hour later I give up.

Instead I add all the numbers together, which comes to 51. Are there 51 wheels on the train, or 51 door handles? Did the train arrive at its hiding place 51 minutes late, or 51 metres from the platform?

I haven't got a clue.

I try something different. I use the numbers to make new pictures. Not of chickens, of things that are also places. Mountains, lakes, famous buildings, statues, fast-food shops.

But I don't have enough numbers.

All I manage is a picture of a sausage burger.

I need to give my brain a rest.

Felix is snoring again, sleeping deeply, and that's what I feel like doing.

Then I see something on Felix's tray table.

The bundle of papers he got from his safe.

They're not stapled together and they're almost sliding on to the floor.

I rescue them. All the pages, each one covered with small neat handwriting.

In English. Mum taught me to read in English. It's still my best reading language. Which would be lucky if I was going to read these.

Which I'm not.

Except for the top page, which has a title on it.

*My Lucky Childhood*
*by Felix Salinger*
*A Memoir*

I'm not sure what a memoir is, but I know what a lucky life is. Felix talked about his in the online newspaper article. It was really interesting, but I wished there'd been a bit more detail.

Here, by the look of it, is a lot more detail.

Incredible.

You know how you're not meant to read other people's private things, but sometimes you can't stop yourself?

Not when you first pick a bundle up and not each time you turn a page?

That just happened to me.

Felix's life is incredible.

No wonder he's still asleep. I'd be exhausted too if I'd had the childhood he had.

All the dangerous adventures.

And all the amazing friendships.

And all the sadness.

So much sadness.

I've just read about Barney, the brave dentist who risked his own life every day to look after Felix and lots of other kids.

And about Genia, who didn't even like Jewish people much, but gave Felix and Zelda very kind good protection, and then got killed for it.

And Yuli and Doctor Zajak and Dov and Anya and Gabriek and baby Pavlo.

And of course Zelda, his special friend.

They all made Felix's childhood lucky in lots of different ways.

Sometimes they made it safe. Sometimes happy. And sometimes, in a good way, they even made it silly. Even with so much war and dying happening all around them, and sometimes to them.

And now they're all gone.

I can't help it, I'm having tears.

I wipe my eyes and make myself help it because at least Felix has me now.

And I've got a job to do.

I look at my screen, at our little plane moving very slowly across a map of the world, to see how much longer I've got left to do it.

The map doesn't have actual words on it, like *Europe*, but I can tell we're about halfway there.

This map reminds me of a map I've just read about. The one Felix and the partisans had in the forest when they were fighting the Nazis.

It was a secret map, so it didn't have words on it either. You had to use numbers to work out where you were and where the Nazis were.

Numbers.

I stare at the screen.

Ms Malinowski is right, I am a bit slow sometimes. But I always catch up.

The map on the screen has numbers.

Lots of numbers.

It has the number of hours and minutes till this flight ends and we catch the next plane.

And the number I press on the remote control if I want to watch a movie.

But I don't want to watch a movie.

I'm more interested in these other numbers at the bottom of the screen.

Which I've just suddenly recognised.

I grab Felix and give him a shake.

He takes quite a long time to wake up, blinking and staring around the plane, and finally at me.

'Sorry, Felix,' I say. 'But look.'

I point to the bottom of the screen.

Felix frowns and peers at it.

I don't think he gets what I mean.

So I show him the chicken numbers on the sheet of paper. Six numbers and the letter N from one chicken, and seven numbers and the letter E from the other chicken.

I point again at the two groups of letters and numbers at the bottom of the screen.

One group has six numbers and the letter N. The other group has seven numbers and the letter E.

Different numbers to the chickens, but grouped in the same way.

Felix's eyes go wider.

'Holy pierogi,' he says. 'Co-ordinates of latitude and longitude.'

I need to check what that means, because none of those actual words are in his memoir.

'Like in the forest?' I say.

Felix looks at me, surprised. But he only does it for a short moment.

He's too excited by what's on the screen.

'N is for North and E is for East,' he says. 'It's the system of numbers and letters that navigators use to find any place on the planet.'

We both stare at the screen.

'Amon must have had a reason to scratch this,' says Felix. 'He must have wanted me to find a particular place.'

'A treasure place,' I say.

Felix frowns.

'The only way to know,' he says, 'is to find out what order our numbers should be in. They're not in any order on the locket, just bits of chickens dancing around.'

I think about this.

'There's something else,' says Felix. 'Back then, I think, co-ordinates looked a little bit different to how they're written these days. When we're on the ground, I'll do some research to check.'

'I'll help you,' I say.

A thought hits me.

'Felix, if we knew which general area Grandpa Amon was telling us about, like which province or district or municipality, would that help too?'

'Yes,' says Felix. 'It would.'

I can see Felix is impressed that I know about provinces and districts and municipalities. If I ever see Ms Malinowski again, I'll tell her she was right, they are useful.

'When we find Uncle Otto,' I say, 'he might have a clue about which province or district or municipality it is. Grandpa Amon might have talked in his sleep or something.'

Felix puts his finger to his lips, and I realise my voice has got loud again.

'Sorry,' I say.

'You could be right,' says Felix softly.

Another thought hits me.

Could Grandpa Amon have said something to Cyryl Szynsky about the locket?

It's possible.

As kids, they were about the same age and in the same town. They might have been friends.

Then I remember something I read just now in the memoir.

About Grandpa Amon, when he was fourteen and in a potato field, punching Cyryl Szynsky in the stomach.

So maybe not. I should see what Felix thinks.

But Felix is very distracted.

Staring at something, frowning. His bundle of memoir, sitting on my tray table.

My tummy goes tight. I should apologise for looking at his personal bundle without permission.

Before I can say anything, Felix turns to me.

And smiles.

'Good research,' he says. 'Well done.'

That's very kind of him, but I think I should still apologise about all the other personal things in his life I read about.

I start to, but I'm interrupted.

A gruff voice booms out.

'Felix Salinger.'

We both look up.

A big man with an unfriendly face, wearing a football shirt I don't recognise, is standing in the aisle staring down at Felix.

'Yes,' says Felix. 'That's me.'

I can tell from Felix's voice he's as startled and scared as I am.

The big man nods.

He's got grim satisfaction on his face.

'I've been looking for you,' he growls.

He's speaking English, but with a very strong Eastern European accent.

Which is very scary.

There are lots of other scary things about this man too. His gruff voice, his unfriendly face, and the football tattoos on his arms.

But the scariest thing is when he leans forward and thumps his big hands on to Felix's shoulders.

**Always** stow your leg rest and tray table before you fight someone on a plane.

I've never had that motto before.

But I do now.

If this man in the football shirt tries to hurt or kidnap Felix in any way, I need room to stand up and swing my backpack at his head.

He's still got his big hands on Felix's shoulders.

'I've got a message for you,' he growls to Felix.

I brace myself for him to say that the message is from the Weasels.

He doesn't.

He takes his hands off Felix's shoulders and, without waiting to be invited, sits down with a thud in the empty seat next to him.

'The message,' he says, 'is from me.'

He pauses, and I'm amazed to see he looks like he's about to have tears.

'Thank you, Felix Salinger,' he says.

He blows his nose on a tissue.

'That's it. That's my message. Just thank you.'

The man doesn't say anything else.

He wipes his eyes and looks at Felix with a very grateful expression.

After a few moments, Felix manages to speak.

'You're very welcome,' he says. 'Sorry about my memory, but are you a patient or family?'

'The way you fixed up my tubes,' says the man, 'after that terrible car smash when I was eleven, fantastic. I can pee straight as a laser beam, three metres sometimes. People are amazed.'

He stands up and holds out his hand.

'Gavin Grotzwicz,' he says. 'Thank you.'

Felix shakes his hand.

Which I hope the man has washed if he's been demonstrating his special ability on the plane.

'Travelling far?' asks Felix.

'Home to Chicago,' says the man. 'After both my parents died in the smash, my uncle in the States adopted me.'

He gives Felix a business card.

'If you're ever in Chicago,' he says, 'and you need storage facilities for concrete-pumping equipment, come and see us.'

'I will,' says Felix, smiling.

The man frowns.

'And you,' he says. 'Where are you off to?'

Felix hesitates for a moment.

'Eastern Europe,' he says.

'Nice,' says the man. 'Enjoy.'

He leans over towards me.

'Sorry to muscle in,' he says. He points to himself and Felix. 'We orphans have to stick together.'

'You're very welcome,' I say, trying to give him a smile that's not too stunned.

'Take care,' says the man, and heads off towards the back of the plane.

I take a few deep breaths, trying to calm my cylinders. And my weird feeling about the man. The way he said to Felix, *I've been looking for you.*

Felix is staring at the man's business card.

'Do you remember him?' I say.

'Not really,' says Felix. 'But it would have been a long time ago, and I had a lot of patients.'

That makes me feel a bit better.

I put my leg rest and tray table back down, and think about something the man said.

Something very interesting.

'Felix,' I say. 'Do you agree that orphans should stick together?'

Felix thinks about this, but only for a moment.

He looks at me.

'Yes,' he says. 'I do.'


Felix offers to answer any questions I have about his life in the memoir.

Which is very kind, and brave. Even just talking about some of it must make him feel very sad.

I ask Felix heaps of questions.

But only about stuff that won't make him feel too emotional.

Guns, and explosives, and sewing up partisans at midnight when your bedtime is eight p.m., and what it's like to live in a hole for two years.

'You don't have to worry,' I say to him quietly. 'I'm not going to ask about your parents.'

Felix doesn't say anything, but I think he's very grateful.

When he was ten he heard that his dad and mum had probably been killed by the Nazis.

For several years after, he had a secret hope that they were still alive somewhere. It wasn't true for his dad, but it was for his mum, and he was able to see her one more time before she died.

It's the most emotional thing I've ever read. Not just sad emotions. Lots of other ones too.

Just thinking about it makes me sit in silence for quite a while.

Felix seems to understand.

Then, without planning to, I tell him about my mum and dad.

'One night,' I say, 'eleven months and twenty-one days ago, Uncle Otto woke me up in my old room at home. He said the police had come with really bad news. That Mum and Dad were dead. I didn't believe him. I thought he was just being a very bad babysitter. Drinking so much of our vodka that he'd gone crazy.'

I stop.

I haven't ever talked about this out loud.

'Take your time,' says Felix gently. 'Only say as much as you want to.'

'I want to say it all,' I say. 'Because Uncle Otto was really good. He made the police take us to the canal. The one where Mum and Dad had gone for a walk after their wedding anniversary dinner. He made the police show us where a person had found Mum's dress and her shoes. And Dad's shirt and his wallet.'

I stop again.

It's hard to breathe properly. But not as hard as it was that night.

I take a deep breath and carry on.

'Too much anniversary drink, that's what the police told us. They said that's why Mum dived into the canal for a swim. And when she didn't come back, Dad dived in to find her. And they both got swept away.'

Felix looks at me.

'In a canal?' he says.

'That's what the police said,' I say quietly.

I can tell from Felix's face he knows why canals are built. It's to make waterways that don't have rushing water.

So people don't get swept away.

'Mum didn't like swimming much,' I say. 'She didn't like drinking much either.'

Felix thinks about this.

'What about your dad?' he says. 'Did your dad like swimming?'

'I don't think so,' I say. 'It made him sad. Before he met Mum when she was in England learning how to be an accountant, Dad came from Africa in a refugee boat. It sank. He had to swim for hours to get to dry land. And when he got there, the old person he was carrying had died.'

I need another pause.

Felix doesn't say anything else either for quite a long time.

I think he's thinking about Dad, like I am.

Thinking how unlikely it is that somebody who can swim for hours in the ocean, carrying somebody else, would be swept away in a canal.

'Wassim,' says Felix. 'There's something I want to ask you. But it's very personal, so I completely understand if it's too hard.'

'It's OK,' I say.

Felix pauses for another moment.

'The doctors,' he says, 'who examined your parents' bodies. What did they say had happened to them?'

That question's not too hard.

I know the answer exactly.

'The doctors didn't say anything,' I say. 'They didn't examine them. Mum and Dad's bodies were never found.'

Felix is silent again.

For an even longer time.

Felix's face is so emotional it's almost like it happened to him.

Then he takes a couple of deep breaths, and when he looks at me his face is calm again, but determined as well.

'Remember the things I told you about Cyryl Szynsky's family,' he says. 'How they probably know a lot of important people. If Cyryl really does want to help, truly wants to, I think there's a good chance he'll be able to find out what really happened to your parents.'

Later, on the second plane, Felix has a long sleep.

I try to watch a movie, but I can't get involved in the story. Not in the way the actors and the music want me to.

There's too much to think about. What's ahead for us. What's happening to Uncle Otto right now. Whether Cyryl Szynsky truly does want to help us and whether Zelda's locket might be able to as well.

Plus I keep thinking about the look Felix had on his face when I told him about Mum and Dad drowning in the canal.

His not-believing look.

I felt the same when the police told me.

But every time I tried to talk to Uncle Otto about it, he got upset and cross. So I made myself stop thinking about it.

Until today.

Until I told Felix, and saw his face.

Now lots of thoughts are nagging at me. Ones that are so secret, I don't even want anybody seeing me having them.

Which is why I need a story blanket.

I learned about story blankets in Felix's memoir.

When Felix was hiding from the Nazis with other kids, sometimes they needed to share stories that were very painful. They were witnesses, so they had to.

They'd sit and tell each other what they needed to tell, privately, together under a blanket.

My story is so private, there's just me under this blanket.

I hope it doesn't look weird.

I don't think it does because on long-distance planes people put their heads under blankets a lot if they can't sleep because of baby noise or toilets.

I can't sleep either, but it's because of my story.

So I'll begin.

Once upon a time, a mum and a dad loved their son very much, and he loved them. They all had great joy together.

But they didn't have any joy at all when people were nasty to them. Which happened a lot, mostly when people didn't like the dad's skin, or his son's.

Sometimes the mum and the dad got angry with the people, which made the people be even nastier.

A few times the boy heard his mum and dad being upset in their room.

Once, the boy heard them talking about whether it would be better for him if they weren't married.

If Dad went away.

I stop the story and take some deep breaths.

It's hard to breathe under a blanket when you're feeling this emotional, and I need to make sure I get enough air. So far the story has been a true one, but now I need even more air because I have to work harder and use my imagination.

Here goes.

What if, once upon a time, Mum and Dad had an idea. Another way to help me. But one where they could both still be together.

What if both of them pretended to have a death without really having one. Instead, they went and lived somewhere secret. Hoping people would stop being nasty to me and be kind instead because I'd be a kid with dead parents.

What if every part of the plan was a secret, including where Mum and Dad live.

Nobody could know.

Not even me.

They knew I'd be very sad. But they also knew Uncle Otto would look after me. And make sure I still went to school. And help me not be too upset. And keep me safe and well until they decided I'd had enough education and they could come and get me and take me to live with them in the secret place.

I stop the story again.

I didn't bring any tissues with me under the blanket and I don't want my sniffing to wake Felix.

I blow my nose quietly on the blanket.

I don't even know why I'm having these tears, because the story has a really happy ending.

Me and Felix arrive back and rescue Uncle Otto. We share the locket with Cyryl Szynsky and together we all find the treasure and Cyryl Szynsky helps us deal with the Weasels.

Then we find Mum and Dad and tell them that they don't need to be dead any more because I'd rather be with them no matter what, plus people aren't always that nice to kids with dead parents anyway.

So no need for tears.

This is a very happy story.

It's about how Mum and Dad might still be alive.

# Felix

**Always** do no harm.

We doctors call it our Hippocratic oath.

Wassim would call it our motto.

It guides our hand each and every time we pick up a scalpel. Or write a prescription. Or go to Eastern Europe with a boy in trouble to try to make things better for him and not worse.

If we get it wrong in the operating theatre or in intensive care, kids can die.

Now I've seen who is at the front of this plane, I'm getting a horrible feeling that the same might be true if we get it wrong in Eastern Europe.

He's sitting in the front row, the individual I spotted soon after we took off. Staring back at us when he thinks we're not looking. Still wearing his Australian football shirt.

Not in Chicago.

Here, tattoos and all.

Gavin Grotzwicz, if that's his real name.

Either he's a lying dog-killing, house-burning Weasel, or he's got a very bad travel agent who sent him from Melbourne to Chicago via a plane to Dubai, a plane to Warsaw, and a small local plane about to land across the border in a country that's not on the way to anywhere in the US, not even for passengers with concrete-pumping equipment.

I tear Grotzwicz's business card into pieces.

'Felix,' says Wassim next to me.

His legs are jiggling with nervous energy as he glances anxiously towards our friend at the front of the plane.

'Is it time?' he says.

'Yes,' I say.

We've just heard that we're landing in seven minutes.

'Are you still OK to do it?' I say.

Wassim nods, tense and determined.

He was very quiet and thoughtful for the last half of our journey, so I didn't disturb him.

But when I spotted Grotzwicz, we had to talk about a plan to get us safely off the plane and out of the airport, and that's when Wassim's energy started to jiggle.

'All right,' I say to him. 'Do it.'

Wassim pauses.

I can tell he's having a final run through in his head of what he'll be saying to the flight attendant.

Then he pulls his scarf even tighter, stands up and presses the call button.

I say a silent prayer to Hippocrates, the grandpa of healing, to keep Wassim safe and medically intact in the hours ahead.

Because if this plan doesn't work, we'll be saying hello to Grotzwicz's Weasel friends waiting for us in the Arrivals Hall.

And I don't think any of them will be interested in doing no harm.

**Always** do no harm, but if you can't manage that, try to do as little harm as possible.

I hope nobody on the plane was having a real cardiovascular emergency when Wassim stood up and said his piece and the crew leapt into action to deal with my pretend one.

And I hope nobody else needs this ambulance right now.

'How are you feeling, Felix?' says Wassim, his brow furrowed with concern as he leans towards me in his seat next to my stretcher.

Delighted that this ambulance is going so fast, is what I want to say. Leaving Grotzwicz and the Weasels back there, baffled and bamboozled.

But I don't.

Two very professional medics are listening.

I give Wassim a slightly painful smile and he pats my arm. He probably wants to give me a wink, but because he's a professional too, he doesn't.

There was a small moment, as the customs and immigration officials were filling out their forms in the medical bay at the airport, when I was worried Wassim was going to give the game away.

'Blood pressure,' he said, eyes big with concern as he stared at the screen I was plugged into. 'Look, it's too high. Felix is in danger. For real.'

The airport doctor was concerned, but only for a moment.

'That's not blood pressure,' said the doctor with a smile. 'That's the time. Fifteen hundred hours.'

I managed not to smile. Just gave Wassim a thumbs up, to let him see everything was going to plan. He gave me one back, but he was shaken for a while.

'Look,' he says now, pointing out the window. 'The old town square. Szynsky's supermarket.'

I can only see the top halves of buildings as we speed past, but suddenly I catch a glimpse of the huge Szynsky sign.

My insides tighten and I hear the beeps speed up on the monitoring equipment as my pulse and blood pressure spike.

I close my eyes.

If Wassim hadn't said, I'd never have guessed we were hurtling across an old town square.

When I was last in Europe, town squares were still paved with cobblestones. Driving across one at this speed would have shaken us to pieces.

Which is how I'm suddenly feeling now.

As I think about another old town square.

Just like this one, but in Poland.

Where I last saw Zelda. Seventy-seven years ago, and just one heartbreaking hour too late.

'Felix,' whispers Wassim. 'Are you all right?'

I open my eyes and realise I have tears on my cheeks. Wassim is staring at me, concerned.

One of the medics pats Wassim's arm.

'It's OK,' I say to Wassim. 'I'm just feeling a bit emotional, being back here after so long.'

'Thinking about people?' says Wassim gently.

I nod.

We ride along in silence for a while, Wassim also subdued and thoughtful.

Probably thinking about people too.

While we're waiting for my heart-scan results, I get my phone out to ring Cyryl Szynsky again.

Wassim quickly reaches across the hospital bed and stops me.

'We agreed, remember?' he whispers. 'No using the phone except when we're on the move. In case the Weasels are tracking it.'

He's right, we did agree that. I'm lucky he's got such a good memory, not to mention such a vivid imagination. We don't want the Weasels turning up here and making more work for the doctors.

'Thanks, Wassim,' I say. 'Sorry.'

'That's OK,' says Wassim. 'Jet lag affects older people more. It's a medical fact.'

I smile.

Before I can compliment Wassim on his bedside manner, we're joined by somebody else smiling.

Doctor Balariek with my scan results.

'That was quick,' I say to her. 'Thank you.'

'Least I can do for a colleague,' she says. 'Had a peek. Congratulations. Quite a career.'

'I've been very lucky,' I say.

I still am. The doctors in this part of the world all seem to speak English.

I wish I could apologise for wasting Doctor Balariek's precious time, but that would be giving too much away. And from the high-rev gurgling Wassim is making with his straw as he finishes his hospital orange juice, he's keen to get moving.

Doctor Balariek hands me the scan results.

I glance at them. Nothing I wasn't expecting.

'Not bad,' says Doctor Balariek. 'For an eighty-seven-year-old with multiple stents and a high-burn metabolism. Just watch the stress, though. We get a lot of older tourists in here who've hoofed it up one set of museum steps too many.'

Wassim stops gurgling.

'It's OK,' he says to Doctor Balariek. 'We're not going to museums. This is just a family visit.'

Doctor Balariek smiles.

Then she leans towards me and slips me a card with hospital phone numbers on it.

'Let the lad's parents have this while you're here,' she says quietly to me. 'Just in case.'

Wassim is watching us over his polystyrene cup, but I don't think he heard.

Doctor Balariek signals to the nurse to get me out of bed and ready for discharge.

'Must dash,' she says. 'Happy visit.'

'It will be,' says Wassim. 'We're planning to make it a very happy visit.'

Wassim hands me my walking stick, and we step out of the hospital staff entrance into the bitter wind to wait for our taxi.

'It's probably safe to switch the phone on now,' says Wassim. 'We'll be on the move soon.'

He looks around to make sure we're not being watched, while I call Cyryl Szynsky.

No answer. Just like when I rang from the airport.

I send another text, similar to the one I sent then.

We're in town. Leaving the hospital. Very keen to see you. We can meet you in the supermarket or anywhere you like.

I send the message, then notice something else.

A voice message waiting to be played.

I move closer to Wassim and turn the volume up, but not too much, and play the message.

'Wassim,' says a voice. 'It's Uncle Otto.'

Wassim's face lights up.

'Stay in Australia,' says Uncle Otto's voice. 'Do not come back. Even if Felix Salinger wants you to, don't do it. I'm telling you as your parent. Please.'

The message ends.

'I'm calling him back,' says Wassim.

He does. There's no answer there either.

But unlike Cyryl Szynsky's phone, Uncle Otto's allows voice messages to be left.

'Uncle Otto,' says Wassim. 'I'm here and so is Felix Salinger. We're desperate to see you. You're not on your own against the Weasels any more. You've got us now, and Cyryl Szynsky, and some treasure.'

I have to smile.

When I was Wassim's age, could I have stayed this positive and clear-headed if my only surviving family member had just told me to go away?

Probably not.

'That's enough for now,' says Wassim with a sigh. 'We're not on the move yet.'

And I don't think, back then, I was as security-conscious as Wassim is either.

'I wish Uncle Otto was on social media,' says Wassim. 'But he hates how people use it to say horrible things about other people.'

'I don't blame him,' I say. 'Doesn't matter. There are other ways to make contact. Let's start with a visit to his place.'

Wassim stares at me as if I've just given him an early birthday present.

'Right now?' he says.

'Right now,' I say. 'A very careful visit.'

'I'll be careful,' says Wassim. 'Wait till you see how careful I can be when required.'

A taxi pulls up next to us and the driver gets out and opens the boot.

'Just the suitcase and the backpack?' he says.

Wassim translates.

I nod to the driver and I'm about to thank him, but then I'm distracted by another car speeding towards us and screeching to a stop.

Not just distracted.

Dismayed.

Inside the car, two men are waving sternly for me and Wassim to get in with them.

Police.

**Always** be polite to the police.

My partisan mother Yuli was a big believer in that. Particularly with Nazi police. She was always extremely polite to them, even while she was cutting their throats.

'Excuse me,' I say in English to the two police officers in the front of the car as we speed away from the hospital. 'Are we being arrested?'

The police officers stay silent. I say it again in Polish. They're still silent.

Wassim translates for them.

'No,' says one of the officers. 'We're just giving you a lift.'

Wassim translates for me.

'Thank you,' I say to the officers.

Wassim translates that twice.

He's starting to look as anxious as I feel. But he obviously knows about being polite to people in uniform. Particularly when you're in their car.

'Where are you taking us?' I say to the officers.

'Your hotel,' says the one who replied before. 'You don't think we'd let you roam the streets after that incident at the airport.'

'Our duty to the taxpayers,' says the other officer.

Wassim is looking even more anxious as he translates all this.

I give him a reassuring smile.

'We might not be in trouble for medical fraud,' I say. 'It might just be for me being old.'

Wassim smiles back, gratefully.

I don't say anything else to the officers. I want to see if they take us to the hotel we're booked into without being told which one it is.

They do. Which is worrying.

I didn't even put the name of this hotel on our immigration cards. All I did was ring the hotel from the airport stretcher to let them know we'd be arriving a bit late.

The police car stops at the hotel steps.

The officer who did most of the talking gets out, signals for me and Wassim to do the same, and pulls our bags out of the boot.

'Stay in the building until further notice,' he says.

Wassim translates.

I try not to look surprised, but I can't help it.

'Immigration have a problem with your travel history,' says the officer. 'When you left Poland in 1946, you didn't fill out the correct form.'

Wassim glares at him, then translates.

I sigh inside.

Next time I fly across the globe on an Australian Air Force bomber just after a world war, I'll do the paperwork myself.

'Your room and the gym and the coffee shop, that's it,' says the officer. 'No leaving the premises till we give you the OK.'

The other officer has stepped out of the car and stands watching us with his arms folded.

'That goes for jungle boy as well,' he says.

Wassim translates. Even the last bit.

I don't reply to the officers.

We grab our bags, and I steer Wassim towards the hotel doors, trying with the gentle pressure of my fingers on his shoulder to let him know how much I wish I had an Australian Air Force bomber handy right now.

And wondering if Wassim saw what I just saw when the police officer unfolded his arms.

How his jacket sleeve was scrunched up.

And his wrist was showing.

With a Weasels tattoo.

As we walk across the hotel foyer, Wassim is still looking stressed, so I don't say anything to him for now about the tattoo.

'Sorry about all that,' I say. 'Me and the police don't seem to get on any more.'

Wassim looks at me sympathetically.

'That's crazy,' he says. 'And not very fair. You're eminent and respected. They should be proud to have you in their car.'

I smile.

'Sadly not,' I say.

'Well,' says Wassim, 'even if they aren't proud of you, I am.'

I smile at Wassim, then glance back.

The two police officers are still out the front, still watching us, still not proud of either of us.

At check-in, while I'm getting out my passport and booking details, I realise Wassim has headed to the other end of the counter.

'That's the concierge,' I call to him. 'I think we have to check in this end.'

Wassim doesn't hear me, so I go over to explain.

The concierge is a young man and he's sitting at the counter, reading. His book has a dramatic cover, with a Nazi swastika on it and a Jewish star. The title is in English. *Jewish Heroes of the Holocaust.*

'Excuse me,' says Wassim to the concierge.

The young man looks up.

'This is Doctor Felix Salinger,' says Wassim. 'He's a Jewish hero of the Holocaust.'

I'm about to explain to the concierge that Wassim's special subject is enthusiasm rather than history. But then I stop. Because when I think about it, Wassim knows much more about history than I did at his age.

The concierge taps his keyboard, glances at the screen, then looks up at me with a welcoming smile.

'Doctor Felix Salinger,' he says. 'It's an honour to have you here.'

'Thank you,' I say. 'Good book?'

The young man looks embarrassed.

'Sorry,' he says, 'but I can't put it down. It's a very personal book for me. In 1943, my grandfather was part of the Warsaw Ghetto Uprising.'

I see in his face how much this means to him. A family connection to the most famous example in World War Two of Jewish people fighting back against the Nazis.

'You must be very proud,' I say.

The young man is silent.

When he speaks again, his voice is quiet.

'I wish I could be,' he says. 'But my grandfather was an SS commandant.'

I give him a sympathetic look.

So does Wassim.

'So please,' says the young man. 'Anything I can do for you during your stay, anything at all, please don't hesitate. It would mean a lot to me.'

'Thank you,' I say.

The concierge gives us a little bow and calls to his colleague at the other end to check us in.

Afterwards, we go to the lifts.

'Poor man,' says Wassim. 'It's not his fault, having a grandad who was a Nazi.'

'Of course not,' I say. 'Good on you for making friends with him. That was very kind of you, and very useful.'

Wassim looks puzzled for a moment.

Then he grins, and I see he knows what I mean.

When you're in a hotel like this, and the police have told the hotel staff to make sure you don't leave the building, a concierge is exactly the friend you need.

'**Always,**' says Wassim as our taxi goes in through the cemetery gates. 'I always come here after school, except when I get detention.'

I'm very grateful to Wassim.

For sharing this special place of his on our way to Uncle Otto's. So I can see his parents' grave.

I also have more of a chance to spot if we're being followed. Going to Otto's is a long shot, but however it turns out, we'd prefer to be the only visitors tonight.

Our friend the concierge was very kind as well, bringing his own car down to the hotel loading dock and taking us under blankets to a taxi rank far enough away from the hotel.

But now we're on our own.

'Here,' says Wassim, pointing to a grave.

The taxi driver pulls over.

Wassim and I get out into the icy dusk.

I pause.

I peer back along the cemetery road.

No lights.

No shadowy shapes of cars.

I join Wassim next to his parents' grave.

Another sad unoccupied memorial.

We stand side by side, shivering. Looking at the two names on the gravestone.

I know Wassim is seeing more than names.

Loving faces as well. And I can't help it, I start seeing faces too.

Some whose graves I can visit.

Anya under a palm tree in North Queensland. Gabriek near his favourite brewery in Melbourne.

And so many I can't because they don't have a burial place that I know of.

Yuli. Barney. Genia. Doctor Zajak. Pavlo.

And, of course, Zelda.

'Felix,' says Wassim.

I struggle to bring myself back.

Wassim is looking at me. He hesitates, as if he's not sure how to say what he wants to say.

I think I know what it is.

'You're right,' I say. 'I'm sorry. I shouldn't be letting my thoughts wander like that. I came here to offer my respect to your parents. For everything they gave you and everything they helped you be, even in the short time they had with you.'

Wassim doesn't say anything.

Just looks at the ground.

I hear a noise towards the cemetery gate.

Still no lights, or movement.

Perhaps a night bird. Or perhaps music from the taxi driver's radio on the breeze.

I should be honest with Wassim. Admit the other reason we're here. The security one.

Before I can speak, Wassim does.

'Felix,' he says softly. 'Do people ever pretend to have a death when they haven't really had one?'

I look at him.

I'm not sure why he's asking, but I know he wouldn't without good reason.

'Yes,' I say. 'People do sometimes pretend that. Not often.'

Wassim hesitates, but only for a moment.

'I think maybe Mum and Dad did,' he says.

I make myself stay silent.

Listening only to Wassim. Trying to ignore the doubting voice in my head. The world-weary old codger I sometimes despair of who keeps forgetting how to be hopeful.

'I saw your face,' says Wassim. 'On the plane. When I said about Dad being a strong swimmer. I saw the trouble you were having thinking how he could be swept away in a canal. Trouble like I was having.'

I see Wassim's face.

Lit up in the gloom with hope.

If he was plugged into a monitor like I was today, his pulse would be beeping fast now.

Very fast.

'So you've been thinking about a different story,' I say. 'Imagining things that might be real. Other possibilities that could change everything.'

'Under a blanket,' says Wassim. 'Like you used to.'

I stay silent again. Watching Wassim sending out beeps of hope into the night.

Sending out some of my own.

That he'll tell me his story.

He does.

**Always** be careful when you visit a car-repair workshop. Sometimes they can be as dangerous as a library.

Wassim and I agree that's a good motto.

We're hoping it won't be dangerous tonight. That just Uncle Otto will be there. Telling himself a hopeful story. How he's better off waiting for the Weasels to come to him, rather than risk a sad and violent ending on their turf.

Just because a story is hopeful, of course, is no guarantee it'll come true.

I tried not to think about that at the cemetery as I listened to Wassim's story about his parents.

The taxi takes us slowly past Uncle Otto's car workshop building, which in the hazy gleam from the one available streetlight looks like it could do with some panel beating itself.

But it's exactly as we'd hoped.

All dark. All quiet.

Not a single Weasel Mercedes skulking in the shadows of the waste ground.

So far, so good.

We must stay careful, though. Avoid attracting attention. No telltale sounds of a taxi dropping off passengers and leaving noisily.

'Sorry,' I say to the taxi driver. 'I must have made a mistake. It must be in the next street.'

Wassim translates.

As we pass another streetlight he gives me a quick smile.

Which is very brave from a boy who knows that after we get out of the taxi and creep back to the workshop and go inside, there is a chance, despite everything, that all hope could be lost.

The first thing we do after we've crept across the frozen mud is crouch outside the workshop and ring Uncle Otto.

No answer. And no phone sound from inside the building.

'What's Uncle Otto's ring tone?' I whisper.

'It's the national anthem,' says Wassim. 'The heavy-metal version. But he switches it off when he's asleep.'

I see that at the front of the workshop, a big roller door is shut and bolted.

Wassim helps me to my feet and leads me to a smaller door in the side of the building.

He points to a small window above the door.

Inside, a blue light is flashing.

Wassim takes a key out of his coat pocket, opens the door, whispers to me to hold it so some street light gets in, steps inside and carefully presses the buttons on a plastic panel.

The burglar alarm stops flashing.

We peer into the gloom of the workshop, listening carefully.

Nothing.

No scowling Weasels launching themselves at us with tyre levers. No Uncle Otto groaning painfully in the darkness. The only sound is from an old fridge somewhere in the workshop.

We close the door behind us.

I switch on my phone torch and use my glove to dull the glare. Leaving enough light to see shadowy detail all around us.

A hoist and a mechanic's pit.

Piles of tyres and other car parts.

A stack of boxes that could be the stolen iPads.

But no cars.

I glance at Wassim, who's watching me.

'Doesn't mean Uncle Otto's not here,' he says. 'He could have lent his car to somebody while he was away.'

I shine the torch around some more.

Against one wall of the workshop is what looks like a very large plywood cupboard.

Big enough to hold several Weasels and their guns.

'I hope there's just junk in there,' I whisper to Wassim.

'That's my room,' he says, offended.

'Sorry,' I say. 'Good room.'

'Handmade,' says Wassim indignantly.

In the torchlight, something else catches my eye, further along the workshop wall.

Rusty metal stairs.

'What's up there?' I whisper.

Behind me, Wassim doesn't reply.

My thoughts are racing. Otto lives here, so his rooms must be upstairs. Which probably means the alarm can be switched on and off from upstairs as well. So someone could be up there right now.

Or a gang of someones.

I find myself thinking of Anya's gun. Wishing it was here, complete with Anya as she used to be, gripping it in both hands, keeping Wassim safe.

But it's not here, and she's not either.

Just me.

I turn back to Wassim. Who is peering up at something on the outside wall of his room. A big hook screwed into the plywood.

'The tubing's gone,' he says. 'Uncle Otto always hangs his rubber tubing here. A big coil of it. He makes his own engine hoses.'

Wassim's eyes are big and panicked.

'Perhaps he's run out of it,' I say.

'He never runs out,' says Wassim. 'There was twenty metres of it last week.'

I don't understand why Wassim is so upset.

He can hardly get his words out.

'This is terrible,' he says. 'The Weasels must have taken it. When you bash a big muscly person like Uncle Otto, or shoot him and he's still alive, you need something strong to tie him up with so you can drag him away. What better thing than twenty metres of superior-grade rubber hosing.'

I hate to admit it, but it's possible.

Wassim grabs my phone torch, pushes past me with a sob and runs towards the stairs.

'Uncle Otto,' he yells.

I hurry after him, and crash into a pile of empty bottles. They clatter across the floor.

Still no sound from upstairs.

Could somebody sleep through all this?

I see they're vodka bottles, so possibly yes if it's Uncle Otto up there. But anyone else would have heard us for sure, and will be waiting for us.

Wassim is running up the steep metal stairs.

'Wait,' I yell.

It's too late. He's almost at the top.

I go after him.

**Always** go slowly on stairs.

When I was a kid, I used to get told that all the time. Now nobody needs to tell me.

By the time I finally stagger to the top of these stairs, I'm gasping and giddy.

Including with panic for Wassim.

I stop and listen.

Apart from the noise of my breathing, all is quiet.

Suddenly torchlight comes towards me.

'Uncle Otto's not here,' says Wassim miserably. 'Not in his room or his office or anywhere.'

He shows me.

In the office, Otto's computer is dark and cold and password-protected. In his bedroom, the bed is unmade and unoccupied.

Wassim gives a loud sob.

'They've got him,' he says. 'I know they have.'

He turns and runs to the stairs.

'Wassim,' I say. 'Wait. We don't know that.'

Wassim doesn't stop.

He clatters down the stairs.

I hurry after him, begging him silently and painfully not to leave the building.

When I finally get to the bottom I'm relieved to see, from the glow of a light inside his little room and a shadow moving in front of it, that he hasn't.

I hobble over to him.

'Can I come in?' I say, knocking on the plywood and pulling the curtain open.

Wassim, surrounded by what looks like more stacked boxes of iPads, is sitting on the edge of his bed, staring at the floor.

I go over and sit next to him.

'Wassim,' I say gently. 'We don't know for certain the Weasels have got Uncle Otto. Let's think about some of the other possibilities.'

I'm about to suggest some of them, but then I see something in the light from his bedside lamp that makes the words freeze in my throat.

The collar of Wassim's coat isn't turned up as far as usual and his scarf is partly dislodged.

On his neck are huge dark bruises. Much darker than his skin. How did I not notice them? Bruises so big and painful-looking.

Before I can say anything, Wassim suddenly turns and looks at me.

'You're right,' he says. 'They haven't got him. I thought they did, but I just saw something and now I know they haven't.'

Wassim pulls his scarf tight, gets off the bed and leads me outside his room.

He shines my torch on to a pile of dusty metal cannisters that look like they've been disturbed very recently.

'Some of them are missing,' says Wassim, 'and they shouldn't be. They've got chemicals in them for flushing out engines, and Uncle Otto says they can explode if you're not careful.'

'And you think the Weasels took them?' I say.

Wassim shakes his head.

'They wouldn't know what's in them,' he says. 'Even if they took the lids off and had a sniff, they wouldn't. Uncle Otto must have taken them.'

Wassim looks at me, his face as close to hopeless as I've seen it.

I don't understand.

Why would Uncle Otto shifting some solvents, even very volatile ones, upset Wassim this much?

Then it hits me.

When you declare war, you need bombs.

Back in Wassim's room, I sit him on the bed.

'Are there any places Uncle Otto might have gone?' I say. 'Somewhere the Weasels hang out. A bar perhaps, or a cafe or a gym.'

Wassim thinks.

He reaches over, rummages in the drawer under his bedside table, and takes out a grubby folded piece of paper.

'The Weasels have got a clubhouse,' says Wassim. 'Uncle Otto used to go there a lot when I was little. He gave Mum and Dad this map, in case he drank too much and forgot how his car worked and they had to go and get him.'

Wassim unfolds the paper.

In the light from his bedside lamp, I see it's a rough hand-drawn map of some streets near a freeway, and in the middle, a square with an X in it.

'Good thinking, Wassim,' I say.

'Not really,' he says. 'Uncle Otto hates going there now, so he never does. These days he drinks most of his vodka at home.'

That's probably better for Uncle Otto, but it's not helping us at the moment.

'Perhaps he might still go there,' I say, 'so he can confront the Weasels.'

I can see Wassim thinks that isn't likely.

As Wassim shrugs, his scarf slips away from his neck again.

I try not to look but I can't help myself.

Wassim sees my eyes on his neck.

We look at each other for a moment.

'Who did that?' I say gently.

Wassim stays silent while he puts the scarf back around his neck and carefully knots it.

Then he takes a breath.

'A Weasel tried to strangle me,' he says. 'I was only listening, but then they hurt Uncle Otto and I couldn't stop myself.'

Wassim looks at me anxiously, as if he's fearing what I'll say.

I don't know what to say.

All I know is I'd have done anything to save him from that. And I want to make sure nothing like that ever happens to him again.

But right now, I don't know how.

So I offer him all I have.

'Let's have a cup of tea and a toasted cheese sandwich,' I say. 'Toasted cheese is good for brain plasticity, so it'll help us work out what to do next.'

**Always** try to have food inside you when the going gets tough.

That's what the partisans taught me. It leaves less space in your guts for fear and anxiety.

Not very scientific, but it seems to work.

The small kitchen above Otto's workshop has no windows, so after Wassim closes the kitchen door, we decide we can safely put the overhead light on without being seen from the street.

While I fill the kettle, Wassim finds half a loaf of elderly bread and some lumps of cheese that are close to retirement.

We sit at the kitchen table.

My legs are still aching from the stairs, so to cut cheese this hard I need lower-back support.

We both start slicing.

Wassim has given me the cutting board, and he's slicing his lump of cheese on a newspaper that was already on the table.

Suddenly he stops slicing and stares at the paper, eyes wide with excitement.

'This is today's,' he says.

I lean over to see.

It's a European football newspaper in Polish, and Wassim's right, the date at the top is today's.

Wassim moves the cheese and flicks frantically through the pages.

'Look,' he says. 'The crossword. That's Uncle Otto's writing. And look, the one clue he didn't get. Real Madrid goalkeeper, eleven letters. Uncle Otto always forgets the names of the goalkeepers.'

I'm amazed, partly by Wassim's very excellent detective work, and partly at learning that Uncle Otto does crosswords.

'Perhaps he'll think of the answer,' says Wassim. 'And come back tonight to finish it.'

I don't say anything.

Perhaps he will.

Wassim has another thought. He flicks back to a different page.

'And if Uncle Otto doesn't come back tonight,' he says, 'look, tomorrow our team's playing at home. Uncle Otto will be there for sure. He never misses a home match.'

I think about this with mixed feelings.

'Won't the stadium be full of Weasels?' I say.

'Not full,' says Wassim. 'The Iron Weasels aren't the real fans. They don't even care that much about the football, just the violence. There'll be heaps of real supporters there as well. We can do that thing you did in the war.'

I'm not sure what he means.

'You know,' says Wassim. 'When you came out of your hiding hole and lived where the Nazis could see you. But they didn't realise it was you because they weren't expecting you to be there. It's called hiding in plain sight.'

'You're right,' I say. 'It is.'

Once again, Wassim makes me smile inside.

His problems might be huge, but all he needs to stay hopeful is an unfinished crossword and an old codger's personal history.

'We'll buy team scarves,' says Wassim. 'And use them to cover our faces until we see Uncle Otto. He'll probably be doing the same, but I'll recognise his coat.'

The more excited Wassim gets, the more I'm thinking it's not a crazy idea. I could tell him about the risks of hiding in plain sight, but I'm sure he can think of those for himself. My job now is to find a way of keeping him safe permanently.

Somehow.

Wassim is watching me. I think he can sense I'm still a bit uncertain.

'I've got something that'll help us,' says Wassim. 'Just in case we need it.'

He goes to a cupboard under the sink, pulls out a box of fruit and vegetables and rummages in the cupboard behind the box.

While he does, I look at the newspaper again.

Something's caught my eye.

An article about why tomorrow's match isn't just any second-division football match. About why the news media will be there.

Which gets me thinking.

And, the more I read, thinking even more.

This could work.

'I can't find it,' says Wassim from the cupboard. 'It's not here.'

I look up from the paper and see how dismayed Wassim is.

'What are you after?' I say.

'Uncle Otto's gun,' says Wassim.

I digest this.

After a struggle, I decide not to say any of the things parents usually say on the subject of kids and guns. For now, we've got more important things to worry about.

Uncle Otto must have taken the gun.

I can see Wassim is thinking the same.

And hoping Uncle Otto doesn't do anything crazy before we find him at the match tomorrow.

There's nothing we can do about it now, except hope he comes back here later tonight, gun still cold, explosive liquid still in the cannisters.

'Never mind,' I say to Wassim. 'While you're down there, grab a couple of those apples.'

Wassim stares at me.

Clearly thinking I'm losing the plot.

A gang of violent killers and an armed uncle out of his depth and all I can think about is fruit.

First things first.

We'll make our tea and toasted sandwiches, then I'll tell Wassim how those apples could keep him safe tomorrow at the match and, I'm hoping, always.

**Always** try to forgive yourself when you've forgotten something important that you should be doing and you can't remember what it is.

If you don't forgive yourself, you'll be cross with yourself all day, which only makes remembering harder, plus you'll get indigestion.

I stay in bed, my eyes squeezed shut in the harsh daylight coming through the rip in Uncle Otto's bedroom curtain, trying to be forgiving.

Until I remember.

I open my eyes, see a radio on Otto's bedside table, find a European news channel in English and wait for headlines on the half hour.

No mention of an explosion or a multiple shooting in this part of the world.

Which is a relief.

Eleven thirty-five. We'll need to leave for the match in an hour if we want to get there early and hopefully see Otto arriving.

Time to give Wassim a shake.

It's eleven forty by the time I've tottered down the stairs and over to Wassim's room.

'Rise and shine,' I say. 'They'll be lacing up their boots soon.'

Silence.

Not even the sound of breathing.

I open Wassim's curtain a bit and peek in. The bed is rumpled but empty.

'Wassim?' I call, puzzled.

He wasn't in the bathroom upstairs, or the kitchen, or the office. The doors were all open.

'Wassim,' I shout, peering around the workshop.

I listen.

Nothing, apart from the old workshop fridge.

A story flashes through my jet-lagged mind. A horror story of stealthy Weasels and violent kidnap in the dark.

I go back into Wassim's room.

This time I see something I didn't see just now. Wassim's pyjamas, neatly folded on the table next to the bed. A kidnapped boy wouldn't do that.

The Weasels certainly wouldn't.

Another story rushes to replace the first one.

A boy who leaves in the night to help his uncle fight a war. After he thinks about how hopeless at wars well-meaning but semi-crippled eighty-seven-year-olds with snap-crackling knees probably are.

My legs have gone so weak, I have to sit down on the bed.

I tell myself that Wassim might just be at the supermarket, trying to find out information about Cyryl Szynsky.

Or in a phone shop, picking me up a cheap replacement phone in case mine has been hacked.

But it's no good.

These stories aren't as convincing as the scary and sad ones.

What have I done?

For three days I've tried to be Wassim's parent. He needs one, of course he does, but not an old fool like me.

I put my head in my hands.

Then I snap out of it.

This is Europe. I've been here before. I've made mistakes here before. One thing I haven't done here before is give up.

If Wassim's out there somewhere, I'll find him.

I just have to think how.

Something on the bed makes a crinkling sound. Something I'm sitting on.

A piece of paper.

A note in young handwriting.

Please Uncle Otto. Don't kill anybody.
We have a plan. Meet us at the match.
Wassim

Thank God. Wassim wouldn't leave this note if he was going off to war.

Which just leaves the question, where is he?

And is anyone else with him?

A familiar sound makes me jump.

A loud click.

A sound I've heard many times in the past. The safety catch being released on a gun.

Except this time, it's not.

It's the workshop door.

**Always** remember to keep breathing.

Partisan training, day one.

'Wassim,' I croak. 'Where have you been?'

I can see from Wassim's face as he comes across the workshop that I must be in a bit of a state.

'Sorry, Felix,' he says. 'You were exhausted and I didn't want to disturb you. I thought I could be back before you woke up. I've been to the library.'

I stare at Wassim, trying to grasp this.

The library?

'I wish you'd told me,' I say.

Because then I could have reminded him that we're in a life-and-death struggle with the forces of darkness, and Uncle Otto is in grave peril, and we have to find him urgently, and we're just not going to have that much time for reading.

I don't say any of that. Instead I tell a hysterical old codger to pull his head in and remember there are other good reasons to go to a library.

Research, for example. Such as finding where the best observation spots are in a football stadium.

'I'm sorry,' says Wassim. 'I wanted to get you something. To help with the treasure.'

He holds out a library carrier bag.

Dazed, I take it.

'Luckily the senior librarian doesn't work on Saturdays,' says Wassim. 'The kind librarian does, and she helped me look these up.'

Look what up, I think as I open the bag.

A small bundle, wrapped in tissues.

'Then,' says Wassim, 'she helped me use the 3-D printer.'

I unwrap the tissues.

A bunch of small, slender objects. So familiar, so good to have in my hands. Cool and hard, but not the usual steel. Something that feels more like indestructible high-tensile plastic. Or resin.

But perfect.

I want to study them more closely, but I can't because my eyes are suddenly full of tears.

Of relief, and gratitude.

'They're to help you feel not so sad about being in another war,' says Wassim. 'I hope they're OK. The kind librarian said it's the first time she's ever printed lock-picking tools.'

**Always** gets the blood pumping, a packed football stadium.

Particularly today, with what we hope to do.

The good protection I hope Wassim will have by the end of this match.

On the way in here, I asked Wassim how he was feeling and he said he was revving on all cylinders.

I hope he can stay as positive as the rest of the spectators revved up around us.

'Any luck?' I say to him.

The match has been going for a while now and Wassim hasn't looked at the pitch once.

Just the seats.

He lowers our new travel binoculars.

'I still can't see Uncle Otto,' he says. 'But if he's here, I'll find him. Thanks, Felix. We're sitting in the best place up here. I can see the whole stadium.'

Wassim goes back to examining the far end of the stadium, seat by seat.

Which can't be pleasant.

Even without the binoculars I can see what's standing on at least a hundred of those seats.

Weasels, yelling and making violent gestures to the visiting team, the visiting fans, the referee, and humanity in general.

And singing some of the most cruel and obscene songs I've ever heard.

Including what seems to be their favourite, because they've sung it four times already, a song about gassing Jews.

Wassim insisted on translating it, even once I realised and told him he didn't have to.

'I know it's terrible,' he said. 'But Mum used to say blocking our ears isn't enough. We have to try and do something.'

Yes, of course.

But right now we've also got a couple of other things to worry about.

One of them is hoping that Wassim is wrong about Uncle Otto, who isn't sitting in his usual seat. Wassim thinks he might have gone to sit near the Weasels.

I don't want to think about what could happen if he has.

Thirty minutes into the first half and still no sign of Uncle Otto.

I keep wondering if I should warn the stadium officials, but Wassim has begged me not to.

He says there's no way Uncle Otto would harm innocent bystanders, but if we say anything about him being here, he could be arrested as a terrorist.

Which is probably right.

Suddenly the stadium goes silent.

The players have stopped running and are just standing, waiting for something.

'Yes,' says Wassim.

It's what we've been waiting for as well.

As important as finding Uncle Otto.

Maybe even more important.

Down next to the touchline, a player from the visiting team is warming up. An official is holding an illuminated board with the player's number on it in lights.

The referee has seen it and has stopped play. Another player, whose number is also on the board, is running off the pitch.

The two players high-five, and the substitute player jogs on to the pitch.

Daouda Ndione, thirty-four years of age.

A man I hadn't heard of until I read about him in the newspaper last night.

In his youth, a very famous footballer in Senegal. One of the most celebrated in Africa. And now in the twilight of his career, pursuing his love of the game with a second-tier European team.

A brave man.

I'm glad to see him on the pitch, because my plan depends on it.

Daouda Ndione is the key to unlocking what Wassim and I hope to achieve here this afternoon.

An unlocking that won't even require the use of the wonderful and precious gift Wassim gave me this morning.

I'm very grateful Daouda Ndione is here, but at the same time I'm worried for him because of what everyone knows is going to happen now.

And it does.

It starts quietly, but after ten or fifteen seconds the screeching noises from the Weasels are echoing around the stadium.

Monkey noises.

Daouda Ndione was expecting it, you could tell from the defiant way he held his head up as he ran on to the pitch.

Now, even from this distance, you can see his struggle not to look down.

Showing us exactly why he's here.

Not just for his love of the game. Also because he refuses to let them win, the Weasels and everyone like them. For his sake, and for the sake of many others.

Including all the Wassims in Europe.

I look at Wassim.

He glances at me, frowning. He was expecting this too, but it's still painful to see it happening in person for the first time.

The match resumes.

Slowly the Weasels' screeching fizzles out.

But everyone in the stadium knows this is only until something else happens.

You can tell from the electricity in the air. The spectators know it, the players know it, the visiting media know it.

Finally, Daouda Ndione receives a pass.

He's twenty metres from the goalmouth.

He looks up at the seething ranks of Weasels behind the goal, and there's something weary about the way he shifts his balance.

Then effortlessly slips past two home defenders and steadies himself for a shot at goal.

Before he can shoot, objects start landing on the pitch at his feet.

Yellow objects, ten of them, twenty, thirty, fifty and more, flung by the Weasels.

Bananas.

Daouda Ndione pretends to ignore them.

He sidesteps a challenge from another defender and shoots.

The ball hurtles from his foot, beats the goalkeeper, but cannons into the perimeter wall just wide of the goal.

The monkey noises are shrill and deafening.

So shrill we can hardly hear the furious whistle of the referee.

Daouda Ndione turns and walks away from the goalmouth.

And now his head is bowed.

This also is what my plan requires.

Sometimes, to protect an innocent boy and his devoted uncle, you can't be kind, you have to be ruthless. But even so, I'm starting to feel sick inside.

I look at Wassim, and he is too.

More than sick.

No wonder Uncle Otto refused to bring him here.

No wonder, as Wassim explained to me, Uncle Otto just kept saying 'when you're a bit older'.

And now, as well as the anxiety of not spotting Uncle Otto, Wassim has had to see all this.

I put my hand on Wassim's arm, but he doesn't even notice, so sunk is he in his painful feelings.

I'm starting to feel sunk too, in doubt.

Always do no harm.

I've tried to live by that motto.

But I brought Wassim here.

# Wassim

**Always** stick to the plan, even if you just want to curl up and have tears.

I bet that's what the partisan freedom fighters taught Felix when he was a kid, and it's what I'm trying to do now.

'Half-time is in five minutes,' I say to Felix. 'We need to get in position.'

Felix hesitates. I think he's pleased I'm sticking to the plan, but he's also looking concerned about something.

'One good thing,' I say to Felix. 'At least this will take my mind off Uncle Otto.'

It won't, but I'm trying to cheer Felix up.

I pat my coat pockets.

'I've got the apples,' I say.

Felix smiles. He organises his walking stick, and we squeeze past the people sitting in our row.

Families of mums and dads and kids.

None of them have got bags of bananas.

But none of them have got upset faces either, and they must have seen what just happened down below us on the pitch.

'Scuse me,' I say, probably sounding cross.

Which I am.

Some of the kids are looking a bit nervous, which at this actual moment, I don't mind.

The next time they eat a banana, I want them to remember what happened to Daouda Ndione.

Felix and I go down the concrete steps, and through a tunnel, and around the outside of the stadium to the place we found before the match started.

The door where the players come in.

I stick to the plan.

I stand back, but in a spot where the security guard in front of the door can see me as I hold an apple and look shy and humble.

Not like a crazed fan or an Iron Weasel.

Felix and I talked about whether he should use his new lock-picking tools to get us in through a side door.

We decided not to. Felix said it's always best to avoid being chased out of changing rooms by angry players who are good at kicking.

Felix goes over and talks to the security guard, pointing at me.

The security guard looks.

Luckily, a lot of security guards in this country are imported from Poland and understand Polish.

As we'd expected, the security guard shakes his head. Felix talks some more. As we'd also expected, the security guard waves at him to go away.

Felix doesn't. He keeps talking.

I can tell he's very experienced at this.

If my plastic knife snaps at lunchtime and I ask Ms Malinowski for a new one, she always tells me to go away and use my fingers. In Felix's job you'd need to be a good persuader in case your scalpel snapped in the middle of a brain operation.

The security guard has calmed down and is listening to Felix again.

Felix is doing dramatic movements with his hands, and the security guard is frowning like he's hearing things he's never heard before.

Probably things about apples and bananas.

He nods, sort of wearily, and lifts his walkie-talkie to his mouth.

Felix waves at me to come over.

You are amazing, Felix.

After we've found Uncle Otto and the treasure, can you teach me persuading?

So I can persuade Mum and Dad to stop hiding.


This is incredible.

Felix and I are walking along the same corridor that actual players walk along. Plus we've got some other very important people walking with us.

Including a publicity lady from the football club, who's talking to Felix while I translate.

She says I'm a godsend.

Which I think is a good thing.

She also says she's very embarrassed about the European TV news people filming the Weasels and their bananas, and she thinks Felix's idea is also a godsend. Filming a local kid (me) giving Daouda Ndione an apple.

She says that will be a very good thing.

The assistant manager of the visiting team plus the TV news reporter and her cameraman all agree.

They're right, it will be.

A very good thing for Daouda Ndione, and for Felix's plan.

We go into the visiting team's changing room.

The players are all sitting on benches, having a drink and spitting on the floor. Except for a couple of them who are lying on tables being twisted and thumped by medical-looking people.

Daouda Ndione is on a bench.

He's not spitting or being thumped.

Just sitting quietly, looking sad, which I don't blame him for.

The publicity lady and the assistant manager go over and speak to him, and they point at me.

Daouda Ndione gives me a long look, frowning, and suddenly I feel very shy and very humble, and extremely nervous.

Then he gives me a smile and a nod.

I give him a smile and a nod back.

I'm not sure if I should nod to somebody as famous as him. The TV cameraman is filming us, which is making me feel even more nervous.

Daouda Ndione signals to me to come over to him. Or does he mean throw him the apple? I think he means that. So I do.

It's a bad throw.

The apple goes nowhere near him.

But he sticks out his foot and flips the apple up into the air and then nods it with his head to another player who catches it on his knee and juggles it from foot to foot and then knees it back to Daouda Ndione, who catches it between his ear and his shoulder.

Everyone is laughing and clapping.

Which is a very good thing. Specially for Daouda Ndione, who looks very cheered up.

So I won't need my spare apple after all.

I glance at Felix, who's smiling.

Then he goes back to talking to the publicity lady and the visiting assistant manager, who has taken over my job of translating. Felix is telling them something, and I think I know what it is.

The publicity lady and the assistant manager both nod. Felix hands something to them.

A marker pen, I hope.

Before I can head over to them and check that everything's OK, I realise that somebody is coming over to me.

Daouda Ndione.

Daouda Ndione gives me a high-five, which is higher for me than it is for him.

Then he looks at me with one of those warm and welcoming smiles that sometimes also have tears as part of them.

'Thank you,' he says.

'Felix,' I say as we climb the stadium steps back to our seats. 'That thing you gave the publicity lady and the assistant manager in the changing room just now. Was that the marker pen?'

I'm meant to know all the details of our plan, but I must have been worrying about Uncle Otto last night while Felix was telling me the pen part.

Felix doesn't answer at first, which makes me worry he might be annoyed I'm asking. Then I see he's just out of breath.

'Relax, Wassim,' he says. 'It's been a lot to take in. All this and trying to find Uncle Otto as well. You were brilliant in there. Your work is done. Just sit back and enjoy Daouda Ndione trying to spoil the Weasels' day.'

I try to sit back.

It doesn't work.

'But they definitely have got the marker pen?' I say to Felix as we sit down.

'Yes,' he says. 'They have.'

I open my mouth to ask more, but Felix does a quick glance at the people all around us, and puts his finger over his lips.

I stay quiet.

I know the plan is a secret, and I wish I'd paid better attention to the details when Felix told me about them last night.

I remember the basic stuff, though.

How the plan is all about good protection.

But I'm wondering if Felix is trying to protect me right now.

From disappointment.

Just in case the most important part of the plan doesn't work out.

**Always** remember something, Wassim.

Disappointment won't kill you.

That's what Dad told me when Uncle Otto gave me a power sander for my birthday and I wasn't allowed to use it because I was only four.

I'm still alive, so Dad must have been right about disappointment, and about power sanders.

But being disappointed does make you feel like somebody's using a power sander inside your guts.

I've looked at every person in this stadium and not a single one of them is Uncle Otto.

Plus the second half of the match started more than thirty minutes ago and Daouda Ndione still hasn't been on the pitch.

I can see him through the binoculars, slumped on a bench with the other spare players.

His eyes are closed.

He doesn't look one bit like a man who's been given a heartwarming and inspiring apple.

I glance at Felix.

He's as disappointed as I am.

And as stressed.

I don't blame Daouda Ndione for feeling down after the bananas and monkey noises.

Plus this match is a dud.

So far neither side has scored a single goal, and there hasn't even been an exciting miss since Daouda Ndione's one in the first half.

The players are still playing hard, but they're looking disappointed too, and so is the crowd.

Even the Iron Weasels have gone quiet.

The atmosphere in the whole stadium is like when you open the boot of a car and find that rats have been nibbling the spare tyre.

Totally flat.

Which means we probably won't be on the news tonight. Nobody wants to see a dud match, not even with bananas and apples.

I sigh.

The Weasels roar angrily.

I jam the binoculars to my eyes and see why.

Daouda Ndione is on his feet, jogging on the touchline.

An official is waving the lit-up board.

The ball goes out of play and the referee blows his whistle and waves his arm and the substitution happens like before.

Except this time there's something different about Daouda Ndione.

He looks just as proud and confident as before, but now he also looks like he's having fun.

He jogs towards the Weasels and doesn't stop until he's right up their end of the pitch.

I wait for the bananas.

There aren't any.

The Weasels must have run out. But they haven't run out of monkey noises. They're screeching like a thousand worn-out brakes.

Daouda Ndione gives the Weasels a big grin.

He reaches under his shirt and pulls something out, round and red, and holds it up to them.

The apple.

The screeching brakes explode with even more furious noise. If they were in an actual car, they'd be red-hot and spewing sparks.

Daouda Ndione takes a big bite of the apple.

Then he tosses it to an assistant referee, turns away from the screeching Weasels, and jogs down the pitch to his striker's position at the other end.

Felix and I share a grin.

Play starts again.

Instantly Daouda Ndione is on fire. In a good way. Chasing the ball, cutting off passes, setting up attacks, having near misses, jumping up with a smile every time his opponents kick his feet out from under him.

He's nearly thirty-five years old. You wouldn't believe this was possible with a player that elderly, not unless you were seeing it with your own eyes.

Felix is seeing it.

He's on his feet, cheering and whistling.

The home supporters all around us are giving Felix strange looks and whispering to each other.

On the pitch, the home players look worried. They're playing like they've decided to go for a nil–nil draw. Doing not-sharesies with the ball, trying to keep it among themselves, desperate to use up the last minutes of the match.

Daouda Ndione sprints straight into a clump of them, and comes out with the ball.

His feet make patterns you can't take your eyes off. He magics the ball past the opposition players so fast it's like they're stacks of old tyres, the ones Uncle Otto grows cabbages in.

The last few defenders get into position and go tense in the shoulders like you do for a very big special effort.

They needn't have bothered.

Daouda Ndione shoots on the run.

It takes everyone a few blinks to realise the ball's in the net.

You've never heard monkey noises stop so fast.

Delighted team mates jump all over Daouda Ndione, but he wriggles out from under them.

And does exactly what Felix hoped he would.

He looks up to the back row of the stadium, where me and Felix are on our feet, and raises his hand to us.

And then does something even more amazing.

Pulls up his football shirt so everyone can see the white t-shirt he's wearing underneath. With two words on it. Written in black marker pen.

FOR WASSIM

I see it first through the binoculars, but then the whole stadium erupts with noise and I look up and see Daouda Ndione and his t-shirt on the huge screens at each end of the ground.

And then on those screens, me and Felix.

Waving thank you to Daouda Ndione.

Thousands of people are watching us.

Some of them are cheering, some are booing, some are whistling, some are shouting things.

The Weasels are using very bad language.

Me and Felix don't care.

We grin at each other.

Felix's plan has worked.

People will remember that we were here. With the Weasels yelling all those threatening things at us. So if we disappear, or even just get hurt, people will know exactly who did it.

And any moment now, that fact will be dawning on the Weasels.

It gets even better.

As soon as the match has ended and the visiting supporters have started celebrating, the TV reporter finds us and tells us she'd like to do an interview.

Me and Felix nod happily.

She takes us up in a lift to another part of the stadium, a big room with big windows and a view of everything except, sadly, Uncle Otto.

The cameraman sets up his camera and the reporter starts the interview.

We do it in English.

That's best, the reporter explains, because then the interview will be translated into the language of each country it's shown in.

I tell her I'm very glad I met Felix, because he's amazing and kind. And I tell her I can't wait to introduce him to Uncle Otto, who's been getting a lot of threats from a gang of violent criminals who pretend to be football supporters.

Felix tells the reporter he's very glad he met me too. And how it encouraged him to come back to Eastern Europe after all these years and accept Mr Cyryl Szynsky's kind offer of working together to give good protection from racist thugs to children and their families.

Then Felix does something I wasn't expecting.

He gently unbuttons my coat collar and pushes my scarf down and points to my neck.

'This is what they do,' he says to the camera. 'The racist thugs. Or as they prefer to be called, the Iron Weasels.'

It feels a bit embarrassing to have the whole of Europe looking at my neck, but I understand why Felix did it, specially when I see how shocked and concerned the reporter and the cameraman are.

The reporter thanks us, and also sends thanks to Daouda Ndione, and explains to the viewers that he can't be in the interview because his team's bus had to leave. She praises his skill and bravery and the way he encourages people to eat more Eastern European apples.

Felix and I have to do our answers a few times until the reporter is happy with the recording.

Then the cameraman takes some shots of us looking down at the stadium, which is empty now. Even the Weasels have finished fighting and gone.

'This'll be on TV news channels across Europe in a couple of hours,' says the reporter. 'And online even sooner.'

The reporter and the cameraman take us to the carpark outside the stadium and thank us and say a quick goodbye because they've got to dash off and cover a street march in the town centre.

Felix gets out his phone to call a taxi.

We've decided to go back to Uncle Otto's. We're hoping he'll turn up there after seeing the news.

'Are you OK?' Felix says to me.

I think he can see I'm a bit dazed by everything that's happened this afternoon.

But in a good way. Except for one thing.

I am wondering if I should have said something in the interview about Mum and Dad. Appealed to them publicly to get in touch.

But I think they'd probably want our reunion to be more private.

When they see us on the news tonight, they can contact Uncle Otto and meet up with us without the glare of the media.

I give Felix a smile.

'Very OK, thanks,' I say happily.

I hear a vehicle approaching behind us in the dusk. Quite fast.

Which I think is a very quick taxi service until I remember that Felix hasn't even rung one yet.

I have a jab of panic.

Did the police on duty in the stadium tell the other police about us? The ones who want to keep us under hotel arrest.

We turn round.

It's not a police car.

It's a very shiny black Mercedes AMG S-Class sedan. Which stops next to us.

The driver's window slides down.

A man in the driver's seat smiles at us.

He's about Uncle Otto's age, but everything else about him is very different to Uncle Otto.

He's wearing a smart suit. And there's no stubble on his cheeks. And he's got hair, wavy and white.

'Welcome,' he says in Polish. 'Please, get in, both of you. Mr Cyryl Szynsky is looking forward to seeing you very much.'

I can see Felix is surprised for a moment, then he smiles back at the man.

'Thank you,' he says. 'That's very kind.'

I don't smile.

I'm frozen with shock.

The man's voice.

I recognise it.

It's the grating and whiny crankshaft voice.

The one that sounds like it's doing damage to an engine. The one I heard through Uncle Otto's office door, threatening to do damage to Uncle Otto.

And me.

**Always** know when to run and when not to.

My friend Jafari taught me that motto.

But then he got it wrong and now he's in a child-correction facility.

Me and Felix decide not to run.

We'd be mad to. All we've got is our feet and a walking stick. The man with the crankshaft voice and the shiny Mercedes AMG S-Class sedan has got a 500-horsepower V8 engine. And somebody sitting next to him.

Who I recognise with a shudder.

Gavin Grotzwicz from the plane.

So far the crankshaft man doesn't seem to have recognised me. Some people are like that. To them, all brown boys look the same.

We wait by the car as Gavin Grotzwicz gets out.

I try not to feel too scared. I remind myself I'm with somebody who's a known genius at making plans work, specially plans to keep us safe.

Felix gives my arm a squeeze.

I give him a quick smile.

I think we're both hoping the same thing. That whatever's going on here, Cyryl Szynsky will help sort it out.

But for now Felix quickly gives me his phone to hide, in case Gavin Grotzwicz searches us.

Which he does.

In my coat pockets he finds our binoculars and the spare apple. But not where I've put the phone.

He takes a bite of the apple.

'Mmmm,' he says. 'Fresh from the jungle.'

Then he searches Felix's coat pockets and pulls out a bundle of tissues. The ones the lock-picks are wrapped in.

I see Felix thinking fast.

He gives a big wet sneeze and a big wet cough.

Gavin Grotzwicz looks revolted and pushes the tissue bundle back into Felix's hands.

A terrible thought hits me.

Was Gavin Grotzwicz one of the Weasels who killed Jumble?

If Felix thinks of that, and loses his temper, he could end up getting badly hurt.

Better if Felix decides Gavin Grotzwicz is just an employee who Cyryl Szynsky sent to Australia to make sure we got here safely. And who is picking us up in an AMG S-Class Mercedes.

I try to think of something to say to Felix, to get him used to that thought, just for now.

'Very nice car,' I say.

Felix is good with words, so I think it helps.

Gavin Grotzwicz opens the back door of the car and signals for me and Felix to get in. We don't have any choice because of the way he does it.

With a gun.

When we're sitting in the back with our seat belts on, Felix leans forward.

'Just so I'm clear about this,' he says to the man at the wheel. 'You work for Cyryl Szynsky?'

'No,' says the man in his crankshaft voice. 'Please forgive me. I should have introduced myself. I'm Kcruk Szynsky, the son of Cyryl Szynsky.'

I stare at him in horror.

My brain is going on all cylinders. As I think about what this could mean for us.

None of it good.

I glance at Felix. His face is very tense.

We're both feeling a bit less hopeful than we were a few seconds ago.


Kcruk Szynsky won't say where he's taking us, but I can see we're going through the centre of town.

In the main square, as we get near the Szynsky supermarket, the car has to slow down because there are hundreds of people marching.

Families mostly. With national flags.

Walking slowly, singing and chanting about how proud they are of the wonderful history of our nation, and how God is proud of it too.

The marchers aren't angry or worked up. It's not really a demonstration, more a bit of showing off by law-abiding citizens about how much they like our country and God and being good.

Which isn't good for me and Felix.

We could jump out of the car at this speed.

But these don't really look like the sort of people who'd know what to do if we told them we were being kidnapped by armed men.

So we stay where we are.

Kcruk Szynsky glares out the window.

'Look at all those fools,' he says. 'Stupid sheep. They'd be going nowhere if they didn't have us pushing them. Doing the work for them. Creating the future of their nation.'

I don't exactly know what he means, but I don't think he's talking about his supermarkets.

We're driving towards the back of the march now, and suddenly I do see what he means.

At the back is a group of Iron Weasels.

They've got the same flags as the rest of the marchers, and they're chanting the same things, but with angry voices and fists pumping, waving banners with horrible slogans on them about people who live here but weren't born here.

And about some people, like me, who were.

Kcruk Szynsky puts his window down and yells at the Weasels.

'If those windows get broken,' he says, pointing to his supermarket ahead of them, 'you're dead.'

Two of the Weasels come over to the car.

'We're on it, boss,' says one.

'Make sure you tell the others,' says Kcruk Szynsky. 'Or I'll fine them until they wish they'd never joined up. You, get in.'

One of the Weasels gets into the car next to Felix, undoing Felix's seat belt and squeezing him over towards me.

Kcruk Szynsky drives on.

Away from the supermarket.

I stare out at the darkness, stunned.

Cyryl Szynsky's son doesn't just hang out with the Weasels, he's the boss of them.

I don't look at Felix.

I can't bear to see how disappointed and worried he must be. Not when I don't know how to help him feel any better.

**Always** try to keep a clear head when you're being pushed by a rude Weasel across a muddy car-park towards a dirty concrete building in a grubby industrial area next to a noisy freeway.

If you let your head go fuzzy with panic, that's no help to Felix.

I look at Felix to let him know I'm on it.

He's being pushed too, by Gavin Grotzwicz and Kcruk Szynsky.

Sometimes he staggers in the dazzle from the freeway cars, but he uses his walking stick to stay on his feet.

'Stop pushing him,' I say.

Kcruk Szynsky glares at me.

'I wouldn't stick your neck out again,' he says. 'You were lucky last time.'

I wasn't lucky, I want to say, I've got a strong neck. But I'm sure Felix would prefer no squabbling now, so I stay quiet.

We're almost at the dirty concrete building, so I concentrate on gathering useful information.

The building is small with a rusty metal door. I think it might be the Weasels' clubhouse because the door has got their logo scratched on it.

Then I see something else.

Tyre tracks in the mud. Very familiar ones.

Tracks that can only be made by Uncle Otto's favourite 210/55 American tyres.

Did they bring Uncle Otto here as well?

Is he inside, tied up?

Or unconscious? Or worse?

I feel sick.

But I force myself to be more hopeful.

At least there's no sign of an actual yellow 1969 V8 Chevy Camaro with orange speed stripes.

And other people use those tyres, including some of Uncle Otto's customers.

The Weasel pushes me hard in the back.

'Don't do that,' says Felix.

The Weasel ignores him and pushes me again.

Kcruk Szynsky unlocks a padlock on the door of the concrete building and switches a light on.

Both Weasels push me and Felix inside.

'I'll return with my father,' says Kcruk Szynsky, not sounding like it's going to be a treat.

'Soon, I hope,' says Felix. 'It's freezing in here.'

Kcruk Szynsky looks at Felix and suddenly I see how much he hates Felix and how much he'd like to hurt him.

But Kcruk Szynsky controls himself.

'I think you can wait thirty minutes to see my father,' he says. 'Given that my father has waited seventy-three years to see you.'

The room is empty.

No Uncle Otto.

After Kcruk Szynsky and the Weasels have gone, I help Felix get settled on a metal chair.

He hasn't said anything about the Nazi posters on the walls, so I think he must still be feeling shaken up from all the pushing.

I look for escape opportunities.

The metal door is padlocked on the outside. Felix's lock-picking tools won't be any help because we're on the inside. The nice librarian would be so disappointed.

The walls are concrete and thick.

There are two windows, small and high up.

They're made of frosted glass with thick metal mesh inside it. Both windows are cracked and have holes in them that look like bullet holes.

I stand on the other chair and peer up.

If I use Felix's chair as a battering ram, I think I could break that glass.

But I don't know about the mesh. Anyway, even if I could break it, I don't think Felix could climb that high to escape.

And I'm not leaving him here on his own.

'Wassim,' says Felix. 'Come and sit down.'

I only just hear what Felix says because this room is so noisy. There's the traffic outside, plus a big compressor doing loud chugging and hissing. The building next door must be a frozen Christmas goose warehouse or something.

I carry the other chair over and sit next to Felix.

'Let's just wait for Cyryl Szynsky,' says Felix. 'I'll have a talk with him. Two people in their eighties can usually find something to agree about, even if it's just sore legs. And, who knows, he might be on our side. There's all sorts of things we stubborn old men don't agree with our sons about.'

Felix is so good at staying hopeful.

But sometimes, like he put in his memoir, good protection is about being prepared for the worst.

'Thanks, Felix,' I say. 'But what if Cyryl Szynsky isn't on our side?'

I point at the Nazi posters.

'Then,' says Felix, 'we'll have to barter. Give him something in exchange for our freedom.'

Felix reaches inside his coat, under his jumper, and pulls something over his head.

Zelda's locket on its chain.

We smile at each other.

The Weasels might have had plenty of training in singing disgusting songs, but they're pretty bad at searching prisoners.

'Have you got the notes you made?' says Felix. 'The lists of chicken words and the latitude and longitude numbers.'

I pull the folded sheet of paper out of the slit I made in the lining of my coat.

When Gavin Grotzwicz was searching me, he didn't even look inside it. If you make a slit with a plastic airline knife, it looks just like a natural tear.

'Well done,' says Felix.

I show him something else I have in my secret stash, apart from his phone.

His gardening trowel.

'Hope you don't mind,' I say. 'Treasure isn't always locked away, sometimes it's buried in the ground.'

'Very good thinking,' says Felix.

'And,' I say, 'I made this just now in the back of the car. For Cyryl Szynsky. So he'll see we want to be friends.'

I show Felix a small folded stork.

'I only had your parking ticket to work with,' I explain. 'So it's not as good as the one I made you.'

Felix stares at it.

'You're amazing,' he says.

I give him a grateful smile.

'How's your memory?' says Felix.

I'm not sure why he's asking.

'We need to learn the chicken numbers off by heart,' says Felix. 'In case the Szynskys take the list.'

We both study the numbers and test each other until we can remember them. Well, until I can.

'OK,' says Felix. 'Now we wait.'

I try to take my mind off Cyryl Szynsky and how much of our future depends on him.

It's not easy.

'Felix,' I say. 'You know how Cyryl Szynsky did terrible things to you and Zelda when you were kids. Did you ever do anything bad to him?'

This could be important.

Felix thinks for a moment.

'I bit him on the finger,' he says. 'Quite hard.'

This isn't good.

I've had experience of this, when I was in Year One. People owning up to biting someone, and saying 'quite hard' when what they really mean is 'very hard'.

Felix is looking concerned now.

Best to change the subject. Keep our spirits up by talking about something else.

'Just now,' I say, 'when you were saying about grumpy old men who don't agree with their sons, you said *we*. Do you disagree much with your son?'

Felix looks at me, surprised.

But he doesn't ask how I know he's got a son, so he must remember it's in the memoir.

He thinks for a moment.

'Yes,' he says. 'I've disagreed with Simon a lot.'

I want to ask what about, but Felix carries on.

'Simon is actually my stepson,' he says. 'When I married his mum, he was already seventeen. He didn't really like me being with his mum, and we never really got close.'

Felix stares sadly at the floor.

'Do you see him much?' I ask.

Felix shakes his head.

'Simon's mum died quite a few years ago,' he says. 'Since then, Simon and his wife have mostly worked overseas. In war zones. They're doctors. Their daughter Zel, my granddaughter, has just joined them. She's going to be a doctor too.'

Felix isn't looking so sad now. I try to find something to say that will help him feel even better.

'Are you proud of them all being doctors in war zones?' I say.

Felix nods.

But a bit sadly again.

So I shut up. Except I don't. Because a very big thought has bubbled up inside me and I can't stop myself asking him one more thing.

'So you haven't got any actual sons?' I say. 'Ones who aren't stepsons?'

Felix shakes his head.

We sit quietly in the noise from outside.

There are things I'm thinking, but I don't say them. They're too greedy, specially from a person who's pretty sure he might still have a dad.

And who also has Uncle Otto, who does a very good job of nearly being one.

And anyway, even if things do turn out badly in the future and I need a new father, it wouldn't be fair to ask a person of Felix's age.

So I don't say anything.

Felix is looking at me.

I'm getting a feeling I've had before.

That Felix knows what I'm thinking. And this time it's making him feel even more sad.

No, not sad exactly.

What's that very useful word Ms Malinowski told us about in poetry?

Wistful.

I should say something.

Tell Felix I'm feeling wistful too.

But before I can, I remember the last time I saw Felix looking wistful. On the plane, while he was staring at the word *Schatz*. And thinking about its other meaning.

Suddenly a thought hits me with a jolt of panic.

'Felix,' I say. 'We have to change the numbers inside the locket. Scratch different ones so the Weasels won't get the treasure.'

Felix stares at me.

'You're right,' he says.

I hunt all over the floor, but can't find a single sharp thing for scratching.

The chairs are made of welded metal, so they haven't got nails or anything.

I look at the bottom of Felix's shoes. Some old people have nails in their leather heels.

Felix's are rubber.

Then Felix sticks his hand into his pocket.

'We can use the lock-picking tools,' he says.

'Brilliant,' I say. 'And I'll smudge the numbers on the sheets of paper.'

But before I can, there's a new noise outside.

A 500-horsepower engine.

Revving across the carpark.

Stopping outside the door.

Felix and I look at each other, panicked.

I try to get some spit for number-smudging, but my mouth is suddenly too dry.

Felix takes his hand out of his pocket.

I don't blame him.

Too risky to get the lock-picking tools out now.

Cyryl Szynsky is here.

**Always** try not to stare at somebody who looks extremely weird and unusual.

Specially when they can't help it.

That's just good manners.

Plus, when a person like that has come into a locked room with a very mean son and two Weasels, staring could get you hurt.

'At last,' says Cyryl Szynsky, looking at Felix.

I can't help staring.

Cyryl Szynsky is the most wrinkled person I've ever seen. The only not wrinkled parts are his eyeballs and the long wisps of white hair lying across his head. And his lips, which are pink and wet.

He's also the thinnest person I've ever seen. He's clinging on to a walking frame on wheels with a hand like a claw. I wish he'd use both hands. Perhaps he's keeping his other hand in his pocket because he wants to look relaxed and stylish.

Ms Malinowski's a bit like that.

Felix stands up.

I can see he's having trouble not staring too. But that's probably because he's seeing Cyryl Szynsky for the first time in seventy-three years.

And having painful memories.

'Hello, Cyryl,' says Felix in a quiet voice. 'Thank you for inviting us.'

'We'll see,' says Cyryl.

His voice is wet like his lips, a wet hiss.

Kcruk Szynsky, who was holding the metal door open for his father and the other two Weasels, bangs it shut and locks it on the inside with the padlock.

That's good.

Felix can use the lock-picking tools on it.

Kcruk Szynsky looks at his father, then strides across the room to me.

'Up,' he says.

I stand up.

Kcruk Szynsky takes my chair and carries it over and puts it down next to Cyryl.

'Dad,' he says.

Cyryl lowers himself on to the chair. Still with his hand in his pocket.

'Thank you, Kcruk,' he says.

One of the Weasels takes the walking frame. Which is a relief. I'm hoping the Weasels are here just to carry things.

'Thank you for your message, Cyryl,' says Felix. 'I was pleased to get it.'

Cyryl doesn't say anything.

He doesn't look like he's smiled for about a hundred years. But I get the feeling from the way he keeps licking his lips that he's sort of happy to see us. Or maybe just remembering something he had for afternoon tea.

'My father wishes to apologise,' says Kcruk to Felix. 'On his journey here from Poland today, he was thinking about his message to you, and he fears he may not have been completely clear.'

Felix looks puzzled.

'About,' says Kcruk, 'why he wrote to you and invited you here.'

Felix is starting to look a bit unsettled.

'I'm here,' he says, 'so we can help Wassim. And others like him. That's my understanding.'

'Sadly,' says Kcruk, 'that's your misunderstanding.'

Felix looks even more unsettled.

I'm feeling the same.

'You're actually here so that my father can show you something,' says Kcruk. 'Go on, Dad.'

Cyryl lifts his relaxed and stylish arm so that his hand comes out of his pocket.

Except it doesn't.

His arm hasn't got a hand.

Cyryk Szynsky's wrinkled wrist ends in a stump, purple and painful looking.

Felix stares, shocked.

So do I.

'Cyryl,' says Felix. 'What happ—'

He freezes halfway through the question.

And he goes quiet. Like he's guessed the answer and he wishes he hadn't.

I wish he hadn't too, if it's what I'm thinking.

'That's right,' says Kcruk to Felix. 'Your foul and vicious teeth. Seventy-three years ago. The day you attacked my father like a savage animal.'

Felix tries to speak, but he can't.

I can't either for a moment, but then I can.

'No,' I say. 'That's not true. Biting a finger's one thing, but you can't bite a whole hand off. And Felix wouldn't even try.'

Gavin Grotzwicz comes towards me.

He looks like he wants to hurt me. But Kcruk raises a hand and he just stands behind me.

'Gangrene,' says Kcruk. 'A foul infection, dear Doctor Salinger, that I'm sure you've had to deal with many times. And, at least once, have caused.'

Felix still doesn't say anything.

He's looking horrified.

'Felix has never had foul teeth,' I say to Kcruk. 'He cleans them heaps. And not just by drinking vodka. With a toothbrush.'

Gavin Grotzwicz slaps the back of my head.

I ignore him.

I want to yell at Kcruk about disinfectant. And how if Cyryl's parents had made sure he washed his hands, including his bitten finger, this wouldn't have happened.

But I don't, because in my experience, blaming dead parents never helps.

'Seventy-three years,' says Kcruk to Felix. 'That's how long my father has waited for you to think about what life is like without two hands. Trying to comfort your children. Trying to hold your wife. Trying to protect yourself in fights.'

Kcruk pauses.

He looks at Cyryl, who is glaring at Felix.

'Seventy-three years,' says Kcruk, 'that's how long he's wanted you to see this.'

Felix is still silent.

'But we thought you'd disappeared,' says Kcruk. 'Into the rat hole of history. Until this bright young lad found you.'

I realise he means me.

I feel sick.

And even sicker when I see that Cyryl is looking at me with his pale bulging eyes. And smiling.

'A godsend,' he hisses.

'Listen,' croaks Felix. 'Please listen.'

I can see how bad he feels.

How much he wants to help Cyryl.

He probably knows all sorts of people who can do hand transplants. Here or in Australia or even in Poland if Cyryl prefers.

'No, *you* listen,' says Kcruk to Felix. 'Thanks to your little friend, you're here to finally pay your debt. Which, for vermin like you, I know is unusual.'

'That's not fair,' I yell at Kcruk.

Gavin Grotzwicz slaps my head again.

I get tears, but I don't care.

'You probably noticed,' Kcruk says to Felix, 'that I sent some of my people to Australia. We could of course have snatched you and injected you and brought you here as a walking zombie. But Dad wanted you fully functioning for this special day. So we just gave you a few little prods to encourage you to come.'

Felix is looking at me, and I can see on his face what he's thinking.

Oh Felix, stop. It's not your fault.

'When people don't want to travel,' says Kcruk, 'it's usually because they don't want to leave their dear pet and their lovely house. So we helped you by taking those impediments away. And here you are. All because of your kindness. Your stupid sentimental mush-brained kindness. Towards, of all things, this creature.'

Kcruk smiles at me.

'What a gift it was to us,' he says, 'when that slop-brained uncle of his took him to Australia.'

I stay quiet.

There's only so many innocent people you can defend at once, and I'm saving my strength for when I can get my fingernails into Kcruk's nostrils.

'Please,' says Felix.

He takes a step towards Cyryl.

'Please don't make Wassim part of this,' he says, his voice desperate and shaky. 'Just let him go.'

The other Weasel grabs Felix from behind and drags him away from Cyryl.

'And so,' says Kcruk, 'the time has finally come. For you to repay your debt. A hand for a hand.'

From inside his jacket, Kcruk pulls a large knife.

'No!' I yell.

I throw myself at the Weasel holding Felix.

Or try to.

Gavin Grotzwicz is still behind me and he grabs me and it's like being picked up by those steel jaws at the car wreckers.

'Don't,' shouts Felix. 'Let him go.'

I try to wriggle free.

But I'm weak and clammy, which is how you feel sometimes when you start to think that things are hopeless.

Kcruk stares at me thoughtfully.

'Of course,' he says, 'we could do this differently. Seeing how fond you two are of each other.'

He looks at Cyryl, who nods.

'That little girl you failed to protect when you were a kid,' says Kcruk to Felix. 'The one you let go into town with just a dumb farmer's wife. Dad told me how he watched that girl die with the rope round her neck. Slowly.'

Felix struggles to get out of the Weasel's grip, but he can't.

'Don't say those things,' I yell at Kcruk.

He ignores me.

I can't bear seeing Felix in so much pain. I want to turn away.

But I don't.

I'm going to do for Felix what he's done for so many other people.

Be his witness.

'I see how much pain you feel,' Kcruk says to Felix, 'when I remind you about that girl.'

Kcruk pauses again.

He looks like he's enjoying every part of this.

'True,' he says, 'with a hand for a hand, you'd feel even more pain. But then it would be over. It wasn't over for my father. It still isn't. So I think we need a longer-term repayment plan for your debt. A loss that will cause you extreme pain for the rest of your days.'

Felix has stopped struggling.

He's just staring at Kcruk.

I try again to get to Felix, to be with him, but Gavin Grotzwicz the car wrecker tightens his grip even more.

I can't stand seeing poor Felix like this.

I've never seen anybody look so miserable and hopeless.

But I don't totally get it.

What else can Kcruk do? He's already murdered Felix's dog and destroyed his home. What else could he take from Felix that would cause Felix extreme pain for the rest of his days?

Kcruk is looking at me again.

He comes slowly towards me, holding the big knife in his hand.

# Felix

**Always** this.

In our greedy world, there's always this one last hope when every other chance of protection has gone and an innocent child is about to die.

Offer them all you have.

I do it now. In this concrete room. A plea to the concrete-hearted.

'Listen,' I say to Kcruk Szynsky. 'I can give you more. More than anything you can get with that knife. Something so much more.'

Kcruk laughs at me.

The Weasel behind me grips my arms tighter.

'Cyryl,' I say. 'Please.'

Cyryl says nothing.

I can't bear it. I can't bear what we've already done to Wassim. Even before the knife touches him. His poor terrified despairing face.

Mustn't look at him.

No feelings.

Just facts.

That's what they taught us in partisan training and the same thing again at the college of surgeons.

'You Szynskys,' I shout. 'Look in my coat pocket. Directions there. From Amon Kurtz. A Nazi train. Big treasure. Wealth that makes your supermarket cashflow look like . . .'

What's happening?

So dizzy, I can hardly get words out.

'I'll take you there,' I croak at Kcruk and Cyryl. 'But know this. If you hurt that boy, nothing you do afterwards will matter to me, and you will never see a single glittering . . .'

So dizzy. Breathing getting hard.

No, please, heart, brain, not now.

Give me longer.

Till I can get Wassim away from here.

Kcruk comes over with the knife and cuts my coat pockets. He grabs the locket and Wassim's notes and the bundle of tissues and the paper bird.

He flings the bird and the tissues away.

'We know about the train,' he says. 'We made Amon Kurtz tell us about it before he died. But we couldn't make the drunken fool remember the location. Which, frankly, is why he died.'

Oh no. Wassim heard that.

Don't look at him.

Concentrate on Kcruk.

'Talking,' says Kcruk, 'of fools who died, let's see how you enjoy this next part of our evening.

Watching your young friend hear about exactly what happened to his parents. Right, Dad?'

Cyryl nods, slumped in his chair, mouth open with anticipation.

'No,' I say to Kcruk. 'Please.'

Kcruk hesitates. Looks puzzled. Puts his hand on the wall for support. But only for a moment.

'What we did to those two fools was a message,' he says. 'A warning to European women. Not to do what the boy's mother did. Foul themselves with men like the boy's father. Foul our nation.'

I feel sick.

I wish I could close my eyes and ears.

Shut out all the men who glow with righteous pleasure after killing. A loving couple here. A few air strikes on hospitals there.

'Of course,' says Kcruk, 'our message would've reached a far bigger audience if Otto Kurtz hadn't stolen the bodies and buried them. We'll remind the fat fool of that while we kill him.'

A terrible sound is coming from Wassim.

A sound no child should ever have to make.

Kcruk coughs and holds on to my shoulder.

'But it's not all bad,' he says to Wassim. 'You'll be going to the same place as your ma and pa. And your traitor uncle when we get our hands on him.'

Bile in my mouth.

Is this what shame feels like when there's too much to keep down?

Just facts.

'Kcruk,' I say. 'Tonight's online news. Wassim at the stadium today. Being howled at by your thugs. If he disappears, the good people in this country will know who did it. They'll come for you.'

I hope I said it right.

I think there's vomit on my chin.

Kcruk sticks his face in front of mine. Why are we both kneeling on the floor? Where's the Weasel who was holding me?

'Old fool,' spits Kcruk. 'Do you think the nation cares? One less Jew and one less jungle boy?'

I'm on my elbows, trying to stay conscious.

Cyryl is on the floor too, eyes closed. Kcruk grabs at my neck, but his hands slide off and he keels over on to his side. I don't understand this. The Weasels are on their knees, vomiting.

I see the lock-picking tools on the floor. I grab them. But I can't see Zelda's locket or Wassim's notes.

Just Wassim. On the floor too. Not moving. Please, no.

A crash. The metal door cartwheels past us.

Someone here, with a gun.

Grabbing Wassim. Grabbing me.

Dragging us.

Gunshots.

Blood on Wassim's face.

'**Always**,' croaks Wassim.

He tries to say more, but he can't do it.

Because of how much air he's gasping into his lungs and how much mucus he's coughing on to the frozen mud of the carpark.

And almost on to the feet of the man who just dragged us out of the concrete room.

Who I'm guessing must be Uncle Otto.

'Just breathe,' Otto says to Wassim.

I try to help. I try to thump Wassim on the back, but I haven't got the strength.

'I always knew,' gasps Wassim, half coughing and half choking. 'I always knew you'd find us, Uncle Otto.'

'Breathe,' says Otto, crouching, breathing hard, wiping the blood off Wassim's face.

Blood, I now see, that isn't Wassim's.

It's seeping out through the arm of Otto's leather jacket.

Wassim puts his arms round Otto's big stubbly head and tries to say something else.

More spasms get in the way.

I can't speak either.

Partly relief that Wassim is alive, partly my own mucus and gasping.

I finally manage to thump Wassim on the back. To help get oxygen into him. Which we must do urgently. Now that I know what we were breathing inside that room.

It came from this big yellow car with the orange speed stripe, engine still throbbing next to us.

A rubber tube over the exhaust pipe, the other end of it duct-taped over the bullet holes in one of the concrete building's windows.

I try to remember the approximate recovery time for non-fatal carbon monoxide poisoning.

Very hard to do while you're experiencing it.

But we are slowly recovering, so the gang inside the room will be doing the same, now the door of the building is off its hinges.

'Thank you,' I manage to say to Otto. 'But now we should leave, fast.'

'You and Wassim get in the car,' says Otto.

He pulls a gun from his belt and turns towards the building.

'No,' yells Wassim.

He flings his arms round Otto's belly.

'Please don't shoot them,' he begs. 'They might shoot you first. Even if they don't, you'll go to jail.'

Otto prises Wassim's arms off his waist.

Wincing as he does. More blood oozing.

'Wassim,' he says. 'Can't you just once in your life do what you're told? Get in the car. I'm not shooting anybody.'

He pulls the rear door of his car open.

'Help me here, Doc,' he says.

I swipe food wrappers and an empty vodka bottle and lengths of rubber tubing off the back seat and push Wassim into the car. I get in and tell him Uncle Otto isn't going to do anything stupid. I try to sound confident rather than just hopeful.

Not easy.

I check Wassim's pulse. Much better.

While I do, Wassim sinks back into the seat and closes his eyes.

I see more litter scrunched under him. I drag it out to make him more comfortable.

Except it's not litter.

It's pieces of paper I've seen before.

Wassim's note to Otto about meeting him at the match, which we left in the workshop kitchen.

And the Weasels' clubhouse map, which Otto must have found there as well.

Then I see a third piece of paper.

Handwriting I recognise from the note Otto left for Wassim in Australia.

*LEAVE ME AND MY FAMILY ALONE OR NEXT TIME YOU WON'T WAKE UP.*

Looks like Otto planned rubber-pipe work at the clubhouse even before he found out we were here.

I peer out the back window.

Otto should be here in the car now, driving us away very fast.

Instead he's standing behind it, busy with a pocket knife. Cutting a length off the rubber tube, which he's pulled away from the exhaust pipe.

He goes over to Kcruk's shiny black Mercedes and smashes the butt of his gun against the petrol filler flap, which flips open.

He jams one end of the length of tube into the petrol tank, sucks on it and spits, coils the other end on the roof of the Mercedes, and leaves it gushing petrol all over the car.

And at last thumps down into his driver's seat, smacks his hand on to the car cigarette lighter, revs the engine and drives us away.

But not far away.

In a circle around Kcruk's car.

Halfway around, he pulls the cigarette lighter out of its socket, flings the red-hot coil at the Mercedes and accelerates across the carpark.

Kcruk's car explodes in an arc of flame.

'How dare that mongrel come to my place,' mutters Otto, 'and drink my vodka, and not even tell me he was a Szynsky.'

I stare back at the flames.

Generally, I'm too old and too weary for petty revenge, but not this time.

That's for you, Jumble, I think to myself.

Then I look over at Wassim to see how he is.

He's breathing well, but is slumped against the window, staring at the floor. Too miserable for petty revenge.

Of course he is, what am I doing?

I put my arm round him and think about the good protection I promised him. How I hoped Cyryl Szynsky would help with that. How wrong I was.

'I'm so sorry, Wassim,' I say.

He doesn't hear me.

Or perhaps care.

Of course not. When you've just lost your parents for the second time, it takes more than an apology or a blown-up car to put things right.

I hold Wassim tight.

He looks up at me.

'I'm sorry, Felix,' he says in a small voice. 'I can't talk now. I'm crying.'

He pushes his face against my coat.

His whole body shudders.

I hold him tighter.

**Always** make medical needs the first priority.

Even when your head is full of frantic thoughts about what else you should be doing.

I learned that from Doctor Zajak in a hand-dug operating theatre under a Polish forest while I was helping him remove shrapnel from partisans who were screaming for vodka.

I send thanks to Doctor Zajak now from this car speeding along a freeway.

Dead for decades and he's still helping.

Which is why we've got the car windows open, icy fresh air filling our lungs. And why I'm in the front, holding a grease rag tight round Otto's arm. And why I'm reaching back to check Wassim's pulse every few minutes, keeping half an eye on my own thumping head.

Otto swears.

Just now I told him about his father's secret message in the locket.

'Why didn't the old geezer ever say anything?' grunts Otto. 'If you or me put secret info about a Nazi treasure train in a kid's bauble and gave it away, we'd probably mention it at least once.'

I can't answer that question.

'Are we near a hospital yet?' I say, hoping Otto can answer that one.

Otto hesitates.

'Wassim still asleep?' he says.

I look over my shoulder. Wassim is stretched out on the back seat, eyes closed, breathing steadily. His pulse has been good each time for a while now, so at least he's re-oxygenating.

'Fast asleep,' I say.

'How bad is he?' says Otto.

'Physically,' I say, 'he's in good shape.'

'How about in other ways?' says Otto. 'I didn't hear what went on in that clubhouse, but I bet it wasn't pretty. Did those cracked pistonheads tell him what they did to his folks?'

I nod.

'So he's not good,' says Otto.

'Fraid not,' I say.

Neither is Otto.

My hand is wet with his blood. I grip the pressure bandage even tighter.

'Carbon monoxide,' mutters Otto. 'Not the only invisible deadly poison. There's also despair.'

I'm starting to see why Wassim is so fond of Uncle Otto.

'Hospital's no good to Wassim,' says Otto. 'They'll just give him pills to dope him out. What Wassim needs is his family, and enough cash to stick one up those Weasels big time.'

I don't comment.

A mental-health expert might agree with that, but child welfare would feel a bit differently.

'The rate you're losing blood,' I say to Otto, 'you need a hospital more than Wassim does.'

'I'll live,' says Otto. 'I've lost blood before. It's just a graze.'

The blood soaking through the rag on Otto's arm says it's more than that.

Otto, come on, I want to say. Be sensible. We need a hospital, and then we need an airport. We're all making difficult choices here. Do you think I wouldn't rather be doing to the Szynskys what you did to their car?

Of course I don't say that. I'm a bit shocked I even thought it.

'We don't need a hospital,' says Otto.

'I'm the doctor,' I say.

'I'm the driver,' he says.

I sigh.

But he did just save Wassim's life. If he wants to be boss of his own bleeding, I guess I should show my gratitude and do what I can.

It's his plan for Wassim I'm more worried about.

'Enough cash to stick one up the Weasels,' I say. 'You mean use the treasure?'

'Yep,' says Otto.

'Even if that was a good idea,' I say, 'there's a hitch. We've got the co-ordinate numbers, but we don't know what order some of them should be in.'

Otto digests this.

'We could go to Zaczyn,' he says. 'See if that helps get the numbers sorted.'

I look at him, puzzled.

'Little old mining town a few hours north,' says Otto. 'My dad mentioned it a couple of times just before he died. Poor bloke was trying to remember why it was in his head. We thought he'd had a girlfriend there or something when he was young.'

'And you think . . . the train?' I say.

'Just a punt,' says Otto. 'It's how I do crosswords. When I was a kid, there was lots of talk about a Nazi treasure train. A bunch of Nazi officers hiding it in case they got defeated. So they could use it to build a new Nazi world. Then the sump scum all got killed. My dad told me only one person alive knew where the train was. He didn't say who, but it was you, wasn't it? Dopey blighter gave you the details in 1942 and then forgot them himself. He didn't mention Zaczyn to you?'

I stare at him.

'Not in words,' I say.

This is the most valuable piece of information we've had about the treasure.

Our best chance yet of finding it.

But it's still not where we should be going.

'Otto,' I say. 'We have to think of Wassim's safety. The Szynskys will be juggling the locket numbers right now, and if they ever heard Amon mention Zaczyn, they'll be right behind us.'

Otto doesn't say anything.

'We need to go somewhere that's not Zaczyn,' I say. 'Somewhere we can work out what to do next.'

Otto still doesn't say anything.

'You have to admit that's sensible,' I say.

Otto grunts.

'No, it's not,' says Wassim.

He isn't asleep any more. His head is between the front seats, eyes wide open.

'We can't just leave the treasure for the Weasels,' says Wassim. 'They'll do the same thing the Nazis wanted to do. Use it to build a new Nazi world. Take over everything. Get rid of everybody who's like Mum and Dad and me and you. We can't let them do that. We have to stop them getting the treasure.'

My head is buzzing with reasons why that's just not possible and just too dangerous.

But I can't put them into words.

Not because of residual carbon monoxide.

Because I have to admit Wassim is right.

Cashed-up Weasels and those like them would be a nightmare. Most elections can be won with enough violence or enough money.

I imagine all of Europe's Kcruks in power.

And feel sick, particularly when I think of what would happen to Wassim.

The Szynskys have left him with a gaping hole in his life. Is it fair to ask him to spend the rest of his days hiding in that hole?

Miserable, lonely and in danger.

Wassim grabs my shoulder.

'The Weasels have already taken Mum and Dad,' he says. 'And Grandpa Amon. And Jumble and your house. We can't let them take everything else.'

He is right.

But Wassim is ten years old.

While I'm glad to see him alive with words and energy again, he doesn't really have a clue about the practical aspects of all this.

Move what could be truckloads of treasure?

Find a place to hide it?

Anyway, that wouldn't stop Kcruk's ambition, just slow it down.

I stare at the white lines on the highway, hurtling towards us in the headlights like tracer bullets.

I think of the Szynskys' thirst for revenge. Which will include Wassim now.

Maybe there's another way.

A way of keeping Wassim safe permanently.

A way that works this time.

I'm pretty sure when the Nazis hid treasure, they didn't just tuck it away out of sight. They'd have set up some sort of protection.

Vicious, ruthless, permanent protection.

And if for some reason they didn't do the job well enough, maybe we can lend a hand.

I'm sitting next to a man who knows how to blow a steel door off a concrete building.

That's a start.

Maybe I can help the Szynskys find the treasure after all. Give their greed a chance to unleash its blindness.

Let the Nazi protection do its murderous job.

To the Szynskys, and to me too if necessary.

I know Wassim and Otto are waiting for my reply. I make them wait a few seconds more while I say a silent prayer. Asking for guidance from all the people who've helped me in the past.

Doctor Zajak, for example.

Whose guidance the first time I had to remove an infected foot with a saw was very simple.

*Go for it.*

'All right,' I say to Wassim and Otto. 'Let's try to get to the treasure first.'

# Wassim

**Always** say thank you when a person's been kind to you. Specially if you're heading into danger. You might never get another chance to say it.

I rub the sleep out of my eyes and lick my dry lips and put my head, which isn't aching as much now, between the front seats.

'Thanks very much for saving Felix's life, Uncle Otto,' I say. 'And mine too.'

Uncle Otto doesn't turn round. In the very early-morning gloom I see why. We're going fast along a narrow country road. But he does smile at me in the rear-view mirror.

'You're welcome, Wassim,' he says.

I check Uncle Otto's arm. The rolled-up-t-shirt pressure bandage has a big red patch on it.

'Felix, I say, 'look how much blood there is.'

Felix peers at the bandage.

He touches it gently.

'Pain?' he asks.

'Same,' says Uncle Otto. 'Not bad.'

Uncle Otto looks to me like he's in a lot of pain. But I hope he's just very tired.

He's been driving for hours.

Felix hasn't had much sleep, and I just dozed a bit when I wasn't thinking about Mum and Dad, but Uncle Otto's had none. He said the good thing about a bunch of murdering Weasels on your tail is that it keeps you awake at the wheel.

Felix peers more closely at the big red patch.

'I think it's just a wet blood clot that's broken away,' he says. 'There must be another clot forming behind it, or we'd be awash. Try not to move it too much, Otto, and if there's any sign of infection, we'll use more disinfectant.'

Uncle Otto frowns.

I don't think he likes that idea much.

He swore a lot when Felix used the disinfectant at the all-night petrol station.

Felix did a great job. He bought three of their first-aid kits and six petrol company t-shirts and patched Uncle Otto up really well.

But every patch-up job leaks sooner or later, as Uncle Otto is always telling customers.

Felix turns in his seat and looks at me.

'Good blood alert, Wassim,' he says. 'You can be on bandage watch.'

It's kind of him.

He knows I need to think about other things apart from Mum and Dad.

I check the bandage again. At least there's no bullet actually inside Uncle Otto.

Felix explained that it just sort of sliced through the side of Uncle Otto's arm and continued on. Hopefully hitting one of the Nazi posters in the clubhouse.

'Co-ordinates,' says Uncle Otto.

Felix turns back to the sat-nav.

Uncle Otto's sat-nav is wide-screen and it shows co-ordinates of latitude and longitude as well as speed cameras and vodka shops.

Felix checks the numbers he wrote on his hand at the petrol station. That's when he converted the chicken numbers from my memory into modern co-ordinates. Now he compares the hand numbers with the numbers on the screen.

'We're getting close,' says Felix. 'One digit to go. I think we should head more towards the east. Let's take the next turning to the right.'

Uncle Otto grunts and speeds up.

That's good. He obviously trusts Felix. Except with disinfectant.

The next turning to the right is a rough track.

Felix is very positive as we bump along it.

'This is looking good,' he says.

I'm not so sure.

There's dawn light now, and I can see what's around us. Grassy hills with bushes and big rocks all over them.

Hills with rocks aren't good for trains.

That's probably why we haven't seen a railway line since we left the town of Zaczyn.

'Locked on,' says Felix suddenly.

Uncle Otto pulls off the track and stops the car in front of some bushes.

'We've arrived,' says Felix. 'According to this.'

I lean forward between the front seats and tap the screen of the sat-nav.

'Is it definitely working?' I say.

Uncle Otto looks offended, but I had to ask because of the hills and rocks.

'We tested it while you were asleep,' says Felix. 'We were driving past a little airport. The sat-nav locked on to its co-ordinates exactly.'

I point to the grassy hillside in front of us.

'But that's way too steep for a train,' I say. 'And it's got rocks all over it.'

Felix looks annoyed.

'Let's try and stay hopeful, shall we?' he says.

'Sorry,' I say, feeling a bit hurt.

Felix hasn't been his usual self for the last few hours. Quiet and tense and thoughtful, which I can understand, but a bit snappy sometimes.

I hope he's OK. Is there something he's worried about that he hasn't mentioned?

Felix sighs.

'I'm sorry,' he says. 'We're all stressed and tired, which I'm not helping by being an ancient grump.'

'You're not ancient,' I say. 'Just a bit old.'

I look at Uncle Otto, who nods.

'Here's what I suggest,' says Felix. 'Wassim, we'll go and see what we can find. Otto, if you can get the car out of sight, try to have a nap. You're exhausted, and if the Weasels appear, we'll have to move fast. And please look after that arm. Keep it supported and don't move it too much.'

'Right,' says Uncle Otto. 'Good plan. Thanks, Doc. I've known lots of bigger grumps than you.'

Felix smiles.

I smile too, but I'm worried about them both.

Blood clots aren't good for moving fast.

And Nazi-damaged knees aren't good for rocky hillsides. Specially when your walking stick got left behind in a Weasel hideout.

For a sec I think about begging Felix to stay and have a nap too, and let me hunt for the treasure.

But I see how brave and determined he looks, and I drop the idea.

I'm still worried about them both.

That's the thing about being very tired and exhausted.

Sometimes you think things are going well.

When sometimes they might not be.

**Always** try to be patient when you're on an urgent mission with somebody who can't walk fast.

It's the kind thing to do. It also gives you both more time to look for treasure-train clues.

Felix and I trudge up the hillside, me giving him a hand when he needs it.

The wind is cold and a damp drizzle starts.

'Poop,' says Felix. 'I should have got umbrellas at the petrol station. You could have kept dry and I could have used one as a walking stick.'

'Don't worry,' I say. 'You got Uncle Otto the most important things.'

I put my ear flaps down over my ears, and Felix tucks my scarf more snugly round my neck. He shakes rain off his hat, and we carry on clambering up the hillside.

Felix is panting like a locomotive.

'I think you're right about this hill,' he wheezes.

I look at him, surprised.

Only a few minutes ago, he was the one talking about staying hopeful.

'Now we're doing an official leg test,' says Felix, 'I think it is too steep. Even World War Two Nazis, who were almost as good at engineering as they were at being murderers, couldn't have got a train up this hillside.'

'Don't fall prey to misgivings,' I say to him. 'There are factors yet to consider.'

Ms Malinowski says that a lot when we start to give up in class. I've never totally understood what it means, but it makes Felix smile, which is good.

And even better if it helps him stop stressing his non-replaceable parts about the Weasels.

'Let's see what's over here,' I say. 'There might be somewhere that's a bit flatter.'

I help Felix over to the side of the hill. When we get there, it turns out to be cliff. Dropping straight down into a sort of lake.

'Looks like a quarry,' says Felix. 'Flooded.'

We both stare down at the water.

From the way Felix's shoulders are sagging, he's probably thinking the same as me. How in 1942 the Nazis might have built a railway track across the dry bottom of a quarry, then hauled their treasure train into an underground cavern, then blocked it in, then flooded the quarry.

It wouldn't be umbrellas we'd be needing, it'd be wetsuits and scuba gear and a two-billion-kilowatt pump.

'Let's look on the other side,' I say.

The other side of the hill isn't so steep.

And it doesn't go down into water, just to a flat narrow area full of bushes and undergrowth.

I help Felix struggle down into it.

Nature can be hard to get through when it's this thick and tangled, and I'm tempted to offer Felix a piggyback.

But I don't. Mum used to say a person's dignity is worth more than gold, and I'm pretty sure she'd say that even about a trainload.

We peer around and see we're in the bottom of a sort of valley.

'This is looking better,' says Felix.

But no sign of a railway track.

I pull bushes aside so Felix can have a better look. He squints at the mud around the roots of the bushes and into puddles of rainwater.

'Hmmm,' he says.

He scoops his fingers through a puddle, then stares at them closely.

Is he washing off that very old chocolate Uncle Otto had in the glovebox?

'Coal dust,' says Felix.

When I look more closely at the puddle, I can see black dust floating on top of the water.

'I think this might be telling us,' says Felix, 'that trains used to travel along this valley. Steam trains using coal. Maybe even coal trains carrying the stuff.'

I look around at the puddles and the trickles of rainwater. Now I know what I'm looking for, I can see black dust floating all over the place.

But still no railway track.

Felix uses both hands to grip the long stick I found for him in the undergrowth.

He starts stabbing his new walking stick into the soft mud, pushing hard on it again and again, in lots of different places.

I've no idea why he's doing this, but I'm worried he'll hurt his hands.

'Let me do it,' I say.

'Thanks, Wassim,' he says, 'but I'm pretty sure this stick of yours is getting close.'

He jabs the stick into the ground again.

I see the stick give a sudden jolt, which is what I mean about his hands.

Then it carries on sinking into the mud. Like it hit something hard, and then skidded off.

Maybe a lump of coal.

'Wassim,' says Felix, pulling his stick out and pointing at the place in the mud. 'Can you have a dig and see what's in there?'

I make a pile of leaves, kneel on them, and scoop handfuls of mud away.

The mud is grey with specks of coal dust. For a while I think that's all there is, until I feel a hard object under my fingers. I pull it out and wash it in a puddle. It looks like a big rusty tent peg.

'Yes,' says Felix. 'Well done.'

Felix takes the peg from me and I can see he knows it's not for camping.

'The partisans liked to wreck Nazi trains,' he says. 'If they didn't have explosives, they'd pull out these iron pegs and drag the wooden sleepers away from under the rails.'

I take the peg and stare at it.

'So there was a railway track here once,' I say.

Felix nods.

We look along the valley floor in each direction. We agree that a train on its way to be hidden would want to travel away from the nearest town, rather than towards it.

The valley gets higher in the away direction, but not so steep that a train would burst a boiler.

Not even a train loaded with very heavy gold and jewels.

'This way,' says Felix.

I help him struggle through the undergrowth, following the route the train would have taken.

It's slow and difficult, with lots of creepers and branches that slap us in the face.

But we keep going.

We don't say much, but I know Felix is hoping the same as me. That at the end of all these slaps and scratches will be something to make up for it.

A huge train, rusty on the outside, but gleaming on the inside, and more stuffed with treasure than anything we've ever seen.

Suddenly Felix stops.

'Listen carefully,' he says.

For an excited couple of seconds, I think Felix might have heard the sound of rainwater plopping on to diamond rings.

But he hasn't.

Felix means listen to him.

'There's a very good chance,' he says, 'the treasure will be booby-trapped. Rigged up with hidden explosives. Which you must not touch, or even go near, understand?'

I nod.

I know he's just being careful, and kind, but I think he must have forgotten that I sleep very near highly explosive engine-flushing chemicals.

'OK,' says Felix. 'Lead on, brave and intrepid partisan trainee.'

There are millions more shrubs and saplings, and we struggle through them all.

Until we stumble and almost fall over, that's how surprised we are to find ourselves in a sort of clearing. With coal dust so thick on the ground, not even the tough, face-slapping types of bushes can grow here.

But no treasure train.

Just another cliff, towering above us. With thick ancient ivy growing along the bottom. Higher up, the cliff is stained with bird poo and the mouldy green stuff that grows on damp rock.

Not gleaming even a tiny bit.

I stare at it, disappointed and puzzled.

'Why would a railway line end at a cliff?' I say.

'Perhaps it's not all cliff,' says Felix. 'Let's see what's behind this ivy. But be careful.'

We start dragging the ivy away from the cliff. Some of it is almost as thick as branches.

For a long while, all we find is more ivy. Our arms are starting to hurt and our hands are getting scratched and cut.

I'm worried for Felix. Elderly people's hands can take ages to heal, even with very good skin cream.

I start wondering if I should go back along the valley to see if there's something we missed. A place where the railway track could have curved away to one side.

I don't go. Felix is wrestling with a tangled heap of ivy bigger than him. I help him and we manage to pull it loose.

Behind it, through even more ivy, I see something amazing. Not treasure, but almost as good.

A big jagged rock.

'Look,' I say to Felix.

The cliff above us is smooth. But this huge rock is jagged and split.

We drag more ivy away, not caring if our hands end up like hamburgers.

'Be careful,' says Felix again.

I'm very excited now, but I am careful, because I know he's not talking about skin care.

Slowly, as we pull away more and more of the ivy, we see more and more of what's behind it.

A huge pile of jagged rocks.

Some of the rocks are half the size of a car. The pile is bigger than several big trucks.

Or a train.

The middle part of this cliff looks like it's been excavated, or blown up, and then filled in again with the huge pieces of broken rock.

Which is probably what you'd do to a cliff if you wanted to hide something inside it.

'Get back,' says Felix suddenly. 'Get away from the rocks.'

He grabs me and drags me away.

'Booby trap?' I say, not really sure what one looks like.

Felix points.

I don't see anything at first.

Then I do.

In one of the places where two big rocks are touching each other, in the narrow crack between them, is a thin black wire.

You wouldn't see it if you weren't looking for it.

'Is that all?' I say. 'That's the booby trap?'

'This wire is probably crisscrossing the whole pile of rocks,' says Felix. 'If anybody tries to get through, their kidneys won't see their spleen again.'

I'm a bit shocked to hear a doctor talking like that, but I get the idea.

Felix's face is grim as he looks at the wire.

But also sad. Well, sort of sad, but not exactly. More like something else.

Wistful.

He snaps out of it.

'Don't be fooled by the wire being ancient,' he says. 'That makes it even more dangerous. There'll be a pile of explosive hidden in there somewhere. Slightest movement could set it off.'

My thoughts are going on all cylinders.

About whether the Nazis who did this were smart enough to make another secret entrance. So they could get in and out without being blown up.

I remember what Dad told me once.

He was trying to invent a car that never leaked, so that the car factory where he worked would give him a job in the design department.

Bad stuff hardly ever gets in through the sides, he said. Just through the bottom or the top.

I peer up at the top of the cliff.

Above it I can see a rocky hilltop, even higher than the actual cliff. And I think I can see a way to get up there.

'Doc,' yells a voice behind us. 'It's too late. Haul your butts. They're coming.'

Felix and I both turn.

Uncle Otto is staggering towards us, clutching his arm to his chest and gasping for air.

'Kcruk Szynsky,' he pants. 'Message just now. On your phone. Weasels only an hour away.'

I'm puzzled.

Why would Kcruk Szynsky tell us that?

I can see Felix is puzzled too.

258

Uncle Otto bends over and for a moment I think he's going to throw up.

But he's just looking at Felix's phone screen.

*'Keep your hands off the treasure,'* he reads out loud. *'Walk away now and the kid lives. Your choice.'*

I look at Felix, who is staring at Uncle Otto.

I think I know why he was wistful just now.

*Schatz.* Treasure and also precious person. Are the stories of both those things behind those rocks? Was Felix feeling wistful about never knowing how those stories end?

Uncle Otto is looking pleadingly at Felix.

'Forget the treasure, Doc,' he says. 'We've got to get Wassim out of here.'

Felix looks at me.

A long look. Wistful again.

Then he turns back to Uncle Otto.

'OK,' he says. 'Tell Kcruk it's a deal.'

**Always** thank your ancestors.

Mum and Dad taught me that.

I hear them saying it now as I watch Uncle Otto flop down on the back seat of his car, and Felix gently examine his arm, which is bleeding badly again.

Uncle Otto is one of my ancestors, and I want to thank him for everything he's done for me, including losing blood.

Grandpa Amon is one of my ancestors too, and I want to thank him for what he tried to do for Felix with the locket.

And even though Felix isn't really my ancestor, I feel like he is, sort of. So I want to thank him too, for everything he's given me.

Felix grabs the disinfectant and the last couple of petrol t-shirts he got for Uncle Otto's arm.

Uncle Otto gets out his pocket knife.

'Do what you gotta do,' he says to Felix.

'I'll fix this dressing,' says Felix, 'and as soon as

I've finished, no hanging around. The two of you are out of here.'

Two of us? I want to say. What do you mean?

There are three of us.

But Felix is bending over Uncle Otto, totally involved in vital medical things, and when you're that distracted, it's easy to get numbers mixed up.

I don't want to hang around here either.

But first I want to say thank you to all my ancestors by giving something to them.

I want to find out why Grandpa Amon put a word in the locket that means both treasure and precious person.

All my ancestors are interested in treasure and also in precious people, so finding out the truth will be for all of them.

I wish I could tell Felix what I'm doing.

But from the urgent concentration, on his face, I think he'd say we don't have time right now.

I don't blame him. Elderly people always like to leave huge amounts of time to do anything.

Luckily I'm young.

I crouch down in the front of the car so Felix and Uncle Otto can't see me.

Slowly, carefully, I reach under the seat and pull one of the leftover lengths of rubber tube towards me as quietly as I can.

Good, it's a long piece.

When you're planning a climb, and you haven't got a rope, you use what you do have.

The glove box is open, so it's easy for me to slip Uncle Otto's torch into my coat pocket. There's a pen in the glove box too.

I write a note on the back of a speeding ticket.

*I won't go near the booby trap.*
*And I won't be long.*

I leave the note on the front seat.

Uncle Otto's eyes are closed while Felix wraps the bandage around his arm, concentrating totally on saving his blood.

As quietly as I can again, I wind the rubber tube around my waist under my coat.

I pause to make sure they haven't heard me.

Then I slide out of the car and run towards the cliff.

**Always** carry a torch.

When all this is over, I'll make sure me and Felix and Uncle Otto never forget that motto, even if it makes our pockets bulge a bit.

I'm at the top of the hill high above the cliff now, and the daylight is very bright up here, but I'd still be hopeless without this torch.

These crevices in the rock outcrops mostly only go down a few metres. There isn't time to climb into them all. You need a torch to show you if one goes deeper and turns into a shaft.

Like I think this one might.

This crevice is different to the others.

It has rusty bolt holes drilled into the rock at the edges of it. The holes are empty now, but once there must have been equipment bolted here.

I drop a couple of stones into the crevice and stare into the darkness, listening to them clattering down.

They clatter for a long time.

Under my ear flaps, my ears prickle. Not with cold, with excitement.

I shine the torch into the crevice again.

Hard to see exactly how far down the shaft goes. I can only see to where it sort of slopes off to one side. The torch beam isn't strong enough to show how far it goes after that.

But it's worth going down to find out.

I hold the torch between my teeth, make sure my gloves are on the correct hands and wriggle feet first into the crevice.

I work out the best way to climb down.

In the rock wall of the crevice, there are places below me I can tuck my toes into and places I can grab with my fingertips above my head.

Some of the foot places crumble a bit, so I learn to test them before I put my weight on them. To make sure I've got a strong foot place before I look for a new hand place.

After a while I switch the torch off.

The crevice is too narrow for me to look down properly, so I'm climbing by feel anyway.

I might as well save the battery. I'll need it when I get to the bottom.

Things go well in the dark for a while.

Then I reach out for a new foot place and I don't feel one. My foot wobbles around in the air. My other foot slips. My hands won't hold me.

I plummet down.

But only for a moment.

Ouch.

Both my feet slam on to rock and then skid off.

I must have reached the place where the shaft slants away to one side.

But it doesn't stop me hurtling downwards.

I'm sliding on my back now. Slippery grit and dust under me, making me go even faster.

Sometimes the shaft has a bend, and as I thump and scrape along the rock walls, I'm very grateful for my thick coat and my gloves and my ear flaps.

I never went to a funfair, so I've never been on a monster funfair slide. I always thought I wouldn't like it much, or find it thrilling.

I was right, I don't.

But at least at a funfair, Mum and Dad would have been waiting for me at the bottom.

Here, there's nothing.

Not even rock under me now.

I'm falling.

Plummeting again, into darkness.

**Always** take a moment when you've had a fall.

To see how you are.

And where.

I can't remember who told me that. Probably somebody who had a bad fall and survived.

If that person was able to see where they were after they fell, they must have still had their torch. Mine slipped out of my mouth while I was falling.

I don't try to get up. I stay on my back, and carefully feel around in the darkness.

No torch.

I'm still very lucky. Soft sand under me. Which must be why my bones aren't sticking out through my clothes.

But what's sand doing here?

I've just come down a long shaft through solid rock, deep into the middle of a hill.

I must be in some sort of cave. That maybe once had a river inside it. Or a builders' supply depot.

I sit up.

Ouch. Pain.

Sharp things stabbing me.

Dry, snapping things. Twigs. Small branches. Dead leaves crackling underneath me.

Trees and shrubs don't grow in a cave like this. Some living creature must have put these here.

I've fallen into a big nest.

Or a burrow.

Or a lair.

If I'm lucky, an empty one. I'm hoping whatever built this was scared away a long time ago.

A very long time.

When the treasure train arrived.


I sit very still and listen.

Silence.

I look around me.

Darkness.

I try to make absolutely no noise. I force my breathing to be slow and soft. But my heart just won't be quiet.

Luckily, nothing comes to eat me.

I shiver. The air here is very cold.

But that's not the only reason I'm shivering.

I'm thinking about how I'm going to get out of here after I find the train.

To get back up that shaft, I'd need to be hauled up on a pulley winch with a very long cable. But there isn't one up there. Not any more.

My only other choice is to wriggle through the booby-trapped rocks. I twist around, trying to see them. And, even more important, to see if there are any small glints of daylight shining between them. To show me where the gaps are.

Nothing.

No rocks, no glints.

I don't give up.

Because I remember my secret weapon.

I reach into my coat, take it out of my secret pocket, and feel better just holding it in my hand.

Felix's gardening trowel.

Perfect for digging a tunnel underneath booby-trapped rocks.

Now all I have to do is solve the other problem.

The one about the treasure train.

Where in this place it is.

If this was Felix, he'd stay hopeful and do creative thinking and make up a story about how to solve the problem.

I remember what Felix said. That coal trains might have come here. So maybe this could be a coal mine. And coal mines have lots of tunnels.

If I was hiding treasure in a coal mine, I'd take it out of the train and hide it in the tunnel furthest away from the entrance.

A narrow squeezy tunnel that big brutes like the Weasels wouldn't have a hope of getting into, or out of.

A tunnel that only someone small and skinny like me could go along. Someone who can twist and slide and squeeze and wriggle. Someone with extensive experience of narrow shafts.

And a gardening trowel.

Yes.

Just a while longer, Felix. Hang on, Uncle Otto. I'm going to start looking for that squeezy little tunnel right now.

I stand up.

In the darkness. The total darkness.

My shoulders sag. Who am I kidding? I couldn't even find my ear flaps in this much darkness.

Then I remember what Felix used to do when creative thinking didn't work. He used to ask his favourite author, Richmal Crompton, to help him.

'Hello, Ms Crompton,' I whisper. 'This is Wassim. I'm trying hard to read your book. Will you please help me too?

I wait. And wait.

Nothing.

I sit back down in the total darkness, and I can't help it, I'm feeling completely hopeless. I just want to curl up on the sand and cry.

I do curl up.

And feel something under my shoulder.

The torch.

After I've finished thanking Richmal Crompton, I stand up again and switch the torch on.

And stare in horror.

This cave is tiny. You'd barely fit a toy train set in here. Are all the caves and tunnels around here this small?

If they are, I've come to the wrong place. And all the danger Uncle Otto and Felix are in, it's all for nothing.

Suddenly I feel a breeze.

Not from above, from behind me.

I swing the torch round, and almost curl up again, this time with happiness.

This little cave is a sort of rock cupboard, attached to a much bigger cave.

A much, much bigger one.

Shining the torch ahead of me, I step through a narrow split in the wall, into the bigger cave.

And freeze.

Stunned and dazed. Ditching all thoughts of twisting and sliding and squeezing and wriggling and tunnelling.

Staring up at what's looming over me.

Grim and dark and terrifying.

The Nazi treasure train.

**Always** running away.

With me.

My imagination.

Mr Cziczowicz, the teacher I had in Year Four, was always accusing me of letting that happen.

He'd probably say it now if I tried to tell him about this monstrous thing looming over me.

This grim and terrifying Nazi treasure train.

I shiver in the huge dark cold cave.

Shining my trembling torch up at the huge dark cold locomotive.

I've imagined this moment ever since me and Felix started searching for it. Ever since I imagined what a treasure train would look like.

Shining and glorious. Dazzling and awesome. Overflowing with gold and jewels and precious things. Not just the luggage racks, all the seats and catering areas too.

It wasn't like this.

Hulking and dark, grim and awful, the dull metal of the locomotive the colour of death.

Just one carriage, with cobwebs on the windows. Ancient dirt on the peeling paintwork. Rust the colour of mouldy blood on the wheels.

I shiver again, then pull myself together.

I'm not here for me, I'm here for Felix.

I walk slowly, torchlight wobbling, to the steps of the carriage. It's the scariest train carriage I've ever seen. And I'm not even inside yet.

I climb the steps.

Shine the torch into the carriage.

And stare.

Is there treasure here? I can see things glinting and gleaming in a dull dusty sort of way. Piles of things all over the floor and seats.

But it's hard to see exactly what's there. Because of what else is there. Scattered over the piles, half covering them.

I try to stop the torch trembling so I can be sure I'm seeing what I think I'm seeing.

I am.

I make a sort of sobbing sound.

When I was doing research about Felix in the public library, I tried not to see things like this.

But sometimes I couldn't help it.

The horrible photos of what the Nazis did to people. Old people. Not so old people.

Often kids.

The heartbreaking remains of their bodies.

Their arms and legs and other bits.

Their bones.

Terrible, awful sights that made me turn away with a lot of tears, trying not to think about how it was for them.

But I don't turn away now.

From these hundreds of poor kids.

Their bones scattered across the whole inside of this carriage. And underneath them, piles of things struggling to glint and gleam and shine in the torchlight.

I realise what the Nazis must have done.

Covered their illegal stolen treasure with the bodies of children they'd killed. So if anyone saw the treasure train rolling through a station, they'd think it was just another Nazi train on its way to dump a whole lot of kids who deserved to die.

Which they didn't.

I'm angry now.

But I force myself to concentrate.

To think about what I've come for.

Is Zelda here?

How do I tell? How do you find a precious six-year-old when so many of these poor kids were precious six-year-olds?

Felix loved little Zelda and even he probably wouldn't be able to tell which bones are hers.

I wish I could gather them all up and give them all a proper resting place. But I can't. There are too many and the Weasels are getting closer.

'Sorry,' I whisper to the bones.

I don't say anything to the treasure.

It's not even treasure really. Because who'd want to take it. Who'd want to be rich if you had to push aside the bones of murdered children to get your hands on it.

I wipe my eyes and hurry out of the carriage, back down the steps.

I want to get out of here. As quickly as I can.

No time any more for tunnel digging under the pile of booby-trapped rocks.

I walk towards the rocks, trying to see if there are gaps and where the best ones are.

Up high, I think.

I'll have to climb.

Then, as I get closer to the pile of rocks, I see why I'll have to be very careful while I'm climbing.

At the base of the rocks is another big pile.

Of rusty metal boxes. With hundreds of black wires attached to them.

On each box is one word.

*EXPLOSIVE.*

I take a deep breath. At least I know where they are. All I have to watch for while I'm climbing are the wires.

I turn and take one last look at the train.

I wish I had a camera so I could take a photo for Felix. So at least he could see Zelda's final resting place. But I don't.

All I can offer Felix are my words.

I stare at the train.

I want to scramble away from it.

Get away from it forever.

But before I do that, there's something else I must do. I'm Felix's witness. I need to make sure I forget nothing and can tell everything. I need to remember every detail.

Including inside the train.

I go back, for one more look.

For Felix.

# Felix

**Always** too late.

That's the story of my life.

For Jumble. For Genia. For Doctor Zajak. For Pavlo. For Zelda.

But not this time. Not even if it ends my life.

I crash through the bushes, flailing at them with my bush stick. My legs are weak with terror. My cardiovascular system is struggling. A frantic shout doesn't come easily but I do several anyway even before I get to the cliff wall and the rocks.

'Wassim,' I yell. 'Wassim.'

No explosion.

Yet.

'Wassim,' I shout, sinking to my knees in front of the rocks to save energy for my voice.

I look up at the rocks and at the greenery still covering most of them.

No signs that young feet have scrambled up there, thank God.

'Wassim.'

I only manage a few more shouts, then I have to catch my breath. Which is when I hear it.

A tiny distant voice from the other side of the rocks.

'Felix?'

'Wassim,' I yell. 'Where are you?'

'I'm in here,' says Wassim, sounding so small, so far away. 'In the cave. With the train. I can climb out through a gap. Up high.'

'No,' I yell. 'Absolutely not. You mustn't climb anywhere. Not high up or anywhere. Do you hear me? Do you understand?'

I wait, panting, for him to say he understands.

But that's not the sound I hear.

The sound is behind me.

A click. A sound I know well. The safety catch on a gun.

I turn.

Standing there with an amused look on his face and a gun in his hand and about twenty Weasels behind him, is Kcruk Szynsky.

'Don't fret, dear old Jew-buddy,' says Kcruk. 'We understand.'

The Weasels laugh, their voices echoing off the broken rocks.

They take me back to Otto's car.

Otto is slumped against the front tyre, handcuffed, cradling his arm across his chest.

About a dozen other vehicles, mostly big old Mercedes, are parked a short way down the hill.

The Weasels handcuff me and push me towards Otto. I stumble and slump next to him against the front of the car.

'Sorry,' mutters Otto. 'They crept up on me.'

I don't say anything.

All I can think about is Wassim.

Kcruk comes over and grins down at us.

'Good work with the treasure train, you two,' he says. 'You accomplished in twelve hours what we failed to do in twelve years. Respect. Take it easy now and leave the heavy lifting to us. Top of the pile I think is the preferred way in, am I right?'

'It's riddled with explosives,' I say. 'Ancient wiring, a couple of molecules away from self-destruction. Go too close and you'll be history.'

The very thing I was planning not to tell them. But it's all I've got to keep Wassim safe.

Please let it be enough.

Kcruk looks at me, slowly shaking his head.

'Oh, Jew-buddy,' he says. 'Didn't anyone tell you? Never lie to a liar. Because we're the experts. We learned from the best.'

'I'm not lying,' I say, my voice cracking with desperation. 'Go and look. You'll see the wire.'

Kcruk smiles sadly.

'Already seen it, buddy-boy,' he says. 'Oldest trick in the book. Throw a bit of wire around and the feeble-minded go weak at the knees. Now, please excuse me, I have to leave you, work to do, but Dad will keep you company.'

Cyryl Szynsky appears from behind a group of Weasels. A couple of them are helping him get his walking frame over the rough ground.

'Please, Cyryl,' I say. 'Tell Kcruk I'm right. You were around back in those days. Tell him how when those Nazis did a job, they did it properly.'

Cyryl gives me a cold look and wipes his lips with his wrist stump.

'Please!' I say, my voice shrill with panic.

'I think we can leave this to Kcruk,' says Cyryl. 'He's a big boy.'

'Thanks, Dad,' says Kcruk.

Kcruk snaps his fingers and one of the Weasels hands him a folded picnic chair. Kcruk unfolds it and puts it down a few metres from me and Otto.

'Dad,' he says.

Cyryl sits in it, facing us.

'Thanks, son,' he says.

Kcruk takes his gun from his pocket and gives it to Cyryl, who holds it in his remaining hand as if he's had some practice shooting left-handed.

'Prefer you don't kill them just yet,' says Kcruk. 'Well, not Jew-buddy. But your call.'

Kcruk snaps his fingers again at the Weasels, and they all follow him back towards the cliff.

'Don't,' I scream at them. 'The boy's in there.'

'We know he is,' calls Kcruk over his shoulder. 'Looking forward to seeing him again.'

And they're gone.

I yell a lot more things.

Pleading. Threatening. Cursing. Sobbing.

Finally, Cyryl raises the gun and points it at me.

'They always said you vermin were smart,' he says. 'But I never thought so. You haven't even worked out what's been going on, have you?'

Cyryl looks at me, amused, eyelids pink and wrinkled, eyes as cold as the first day I met him.

'I didn't write that message to you for revenge,' he says. 'Kcruk thought I did, but I didn't. I don't give a rat's scrotum about revenge. I wrote it for him. Kcruk couldn't find treasure on his own if it was stapled to his appendage. I did it because he's my son. And because his vision of the future is my gift to the world.'

Cyryl gives me a sad smile.

'Of course,' he says. 'You wouldn't understand. You haven't got a son, have you? Not a real one.'

I can't speak. Or breathe.

Otto is quietly sobbing now.

Through my own tears, I see Cyryl put the gun on his knees and hold it steady with his elbow and click off the safety catch.

Then he puts his hand in his pocket and throws something towards me. Something that lands near my feet with a faint metallic sound.

I wipe my eyes.

Something gleaming on the ground.

Two shiny keys.

Cyryl raises the gun again, aimed at my head.

'This must be very painful for you,' he says. 'Helpless and hopeless. Imagining what Kcruk will do to the boy here in front of you. As one old man to another, let me give you a way out. Win-win. You get the chance to unlock your cuffs and overpower me. I get the chance to kill you in self-defence. Whichever happens, we've both acted nobly. Our mortal souls remain unsullied.'

On Cyryl's face, I can see exactly what he thinks will happen.

The gun in his hand is trembling, just a little. Partly with old age, mostly with excitement.

I pull the front of my coat over my head and blot him out.

Not so he won't see my fear.

So he won't see my hands. Sorting through the bundle of lock picks. Feeling for the one I need. Slipping it into the lock of the handcuffs. Muffling the sound of the cuffs opening.

No time for fear.

I need several deep breaths to steady myself, but I only take one.

I fling my coat at Cyryl, then the handcuffs.

The coat surprises him, the handcuffs slam into his face, knocking him backwards off his chair.

He hits the ground heavily.

I grab the front of the car and haul myself up.

I know I probably haven't got enough time, but all I can do is try.

'Doc,' says Otto.

He's looking up at me, pleading.

I grab the keys and unlock his cuffs. He heaves himself on to his feet, but then staggers, blood loss taking its toll.

'Come on,' I say.

But even before I can turn and propel myself towards the cave, towards Wassim, I hear a scream.

The distant scream of a grown man.

A Weasel scream.

I'm too late.

I grab Otto and push him, both of us staggering, back on to the ground. I flatten myself next to him, hoping all the bits of us are behind the car.

The ground shakes.

I sob a wordless prayer for the boy who's not my son, but who I love anyway.

Then silence.

I look up, just in time to see Cyryl, on his knees behind his chair, gun gripped and pointing at me, become surprised, then alarmed.

Then, as the universe roars and the rock storm slams into us, he becomes a red mist, then nothing.

Same, I fear, as everything else.

**Always** hopeful.

That's how I'm trying to be, despite everything. Despite the voice inside me saying *hopeless*.

Because without hope, there really is nothing.

Otto and I haul ourselves to our feet, clinging on to the little that's left of Otto's car, our battered good protection.

We stumble towards the pile of rocks.

Which is mostly gone.

Well, dispersed. Rock chunks flung everywhere, small fragments crunching underfoot as we pick our way towards the cave, through tangled shreds of trees and bushes, some still green, some half black and all of them spattered with tiny globules of human cellular matter.

Just Weasels, please, just them.

The entrance to the cave is wide open, huge and jagged and swirling with dust.

Silent now.

'Wassim!' I yell.

So does Otto, over and over as we stumble in.

There it is. The train. Huge and jagged too, and shattered. The locomotive a twisted carcass.

Oh, Wassim.

Behind the locomotive is what must have been a carriage.

Just a chassis now.

Everything that was on the chassis is a carpet of fragments under our feet.

Metal, wood, canvas, and countless other tiny pieces, some struggling pitifully to gleam.

I stare at the fragments.

Crouch and study some of them more closely. Confirm that I'm seeing what I think I am.

Bone.

A few slightly larger pieces just recognisable as fragments of human bone. Small human bones.

Children.

And now I understand.

My whole life has been a journey to this place, and this moment.

Everything, my best and my worst, our best and our worst, hanging in perilous balance as we wait to see which of them will fall and which will rise.

And now I let myself fall.

Knees finally giving up, and other parts of me too, my cheek against the fragments.

Every one of them precious.

I close my eyes.

All I hoped for was to offer my ancient life to protect the life of a single child.

Oh, Wassim.

A sound.

So small and distant and painful, I fear it's just a memory reaching out to torment me.

'Felix,' says the small voice. 'Uncle Otto.'

I open my eyes. Turn my head.

Nothing.

No one.

Just a pile of sand like a freshly dug grave in a small cave off the main one.

Grains of sand tumbling now, with what looks like tiny pieces of train and treasure tumbling too, as a figure with a length of rubber tube dangling from his mouth slowly emerges from deep in the precious sand.

A hiding hole.

Wassim stumbles towards us.

Otto grabs him first, big arms wrapped around him, blubbering joyfully, dabbing with what's left of his own coat at the blood on Wassim's ears, but after hugging Otto back, Wassim says something and Otto lets him go.

Wassim comes to me.

'Look, Felix,' he says.

I see the gardening trowel sticking out of his torn coat pocket. But that's not what he gives me.

'This was in the driver's cabin,' he says.

He hands me the tattered bundled remnants of an ancient linen bag, stained with age, and points to a faded piece of handwriting on the fabric.

'Grandpa Amon's writing,' says Wassim.

I recognise it as the same handwriting I read the very first day Wassim came into my life and we began our time together.

On the fabric is just a single word.

*Zelda*

My hands are shaking too much, so Wassim helps me. He gently unwraps the bundle and shows me the small and perfectly preserved bones.

I'm speechless.

But Wassim's face has fallen.

'I'm sorry, Felix,' he says. 'The bag was empty. So I chose some bones. I know that might be wrong and I understand if you feel she's probably not here. But they could be hers, couldn't they?'

I gaze at the precious bones in my hands, but when I'm finally able to speak, it's Wassim I'm looking at.

This brave boy who's given me so much.

Who'll give so much to so many.

His dear concerned face, his thin trembling shoulders shielding the hopeful heart that is our human future.

'Oh, Wassim.' I say. 'She's here.'

# Wassim

**Always** take your time when you dig a grave.

Specially when you've got a proper spade like this one they gave me.

And specially when an official gravedigger at this cemetery, who is kindly letting me do the digging myself, is nodding to show how much he agrees with my motto.

'Good work, boy,' he says.

I think Mum and Dad agree too.

A warm breeze is gently lifting my ear flaps. The ones they sewed on my beanie together. Smiling as they did and telling me that to do a good job, all you need is good tools and love in your heart.

I think they were talking about my life as well.

I'm glad we decided to wait until spring. The soil here next to Mum and Dad's grave is soft and fragrant, and I know that's what they'd want for Zelda's final resting place.

It's what Felix wanted too.

As I finish digging, Felix comes over, smiling.

'Thank you, Wassim,' he says. 'You've done a very beautiful job.'

The official gravedigger agrees.

'You're welcome,' I say to them both. 'And you're welcome too, Zel.'

'Thank you, Wassim,' says Zel, who arrived from Syria only a few days ago, which is the other reason we waited until spring.

Uncle Otto lifts me out of the grave.

He gives me a squeeze, which makes my bones crack a bit, which I'm really pleased about because it shows his arm is almost totally healed.

'I'm proud of you, Wassim,' he says.

'Thanks, Uncle Otto,' I say. 'I'm proud of you too.'

I am, a lot. The little casket he made for Zelda is brilliant, and all from real timber.

Everyone gathers around the grave.

Felix says some words about Zelda and her life.

We stand in silence for a while, thinking about her. Then Felix and Zel lower her casket on to the flowers in the grave, and we all sprinkle our soil and silently say our own words.

Afterwards, when the others head off to the big tree in the sunlight to get our picnic ready, Felix stays to help me finish.

I let him put the first few spadefuls in.

'Let me, now,' I say when I see him getting tired.

Felix hesitates, then hands me the spade with a smile.

You know how sometimes two friends look at each other, and they know without saying a word that whatever happens in the future, and wherever they go, and whatever they do, even if it's not together, even if there are other friends in their life too, even if one of them falls in love one day and even makes a new family, even if one of them dies, that both of them will always remember this moment and each other, and that the younger one will do everything he can for the rest of his life to be as kind and friendly and brave and hopeful and good at stories as the older one?

That's happening now to me and Felix.

# Felix

**Always** knew, of course I did, that I'd be here one day.

On this side of the sheets.

Not just sitting on the corner of the hospital bed any more, talking to the person in it, letting them know what we've done for them, what remains for us to do, what might happen, always reassuring them that whatever does happen, they will be held safe every moment they're in this hospital, lying in this bed.

Like I am now.

'Fill the room,' I'd often say to them if I knew they had plenty of family and friends. 'As many as you like.'

And often they did.

With flesh and blood, and hopes and memories.

Like I am now.

So many precious faces in this small room. My own dear mum and dad, and so many more.

I think you know who they are.

They know who they are.

Smiles. Nods.

Some tears.

Only a few are here in flesh and blood.

Zel, Ruby, Sheree, Uncle Otto and a boy with dark eyes and curly hair.

Who hands me a sheet of paper, pathology results from the clipboard at the foot of my bed, folded into a beautiful bird.

I smile my thanks to him, my dear new and last friend, whose face is sad now but who I know will fill his life with hope and the lives of many with gratitude.

As everyone here has filled my life.

Deeply and generously and in so many ways.

My ancient body, now barely able to keep the equipment beeping and glowing around me, but so patient and loyal and forgiving for so long, including granting me my final wish, a slow walk up a mountainside to an orphanage from long ago . . . it too is glowing from the love in this last room.

So much love.

Including, of course, from the little girl looking at me with a stern unyielding gaze.

'Don't you know anything?' she says softly.

'No,' I say, smiling.

She smiles too. She knows I'm talking about where I'm going, and that I don't mind.

Thank you, dear ones who have shared my story.

Please remember that while some of you blessed my life with your physical presence, and some of you simply graced my imagination, you were all in my heart.

And there you will stay.

Alive and full of hope.

Always.

*Dear Reader,*

*I'm writing to you from a long-wished-for destination, with a mixture of feelings.*

*I remember the excitement I felt when I first met Felix in my imagination, and also the anxiety.*

*Excitement because finding this brave and loving ten-year-old at last made possible the story I hoped to write. Anxiety because I still wasn't sure if I knew how to write it.*

*We set off on the journey anyway, hoping we'd discover the way. Thanks to Felix, we did.*

*Sixteen years later, as Felix and I come to what feels like the end of our work together, I'm a little tearful, a little weary in a happy way, and immensely grateful for our seven-book friendship.*

*It's been quite a journey, dear Felix. Thank you for taking me with you.*

*And thank you, dear reader, for coming along too. Without you, no journey is possible, and no destination. Because as every writer knows, stories don't fully exist until a reader's heart pulses life into them.*

*When Once was first published, some people found the thought of Felix's struggles a bit daunting. So a special thank you to those who paved the way. Felix's early readers, who took a chance with him and then introduced him to their friends. Thank you as well to all the parents, rellies, teachers, librarians, booksellers and reviewers who did the same.*

As the later books followed, the order I wrote them in went a little awry.

I had started out with a single book in mind, then three, and by the time Felix steered me towards seven, I was all over the place. I am deeply sorry.

Little consolation to those of you who've already struggled through, but the actual order of Felix's life story is:

Once, Then, After, Soon, Maybe, Now, Always.

A geographical note about Always. The story takes place partly in a country in Eastern Europe. I decided not to pick a particular country because my feeling is it doesn't really matter.

Events like some of those that happen in Always sadly also happen in many other parts of the world. Eastern Europe is important to this story because it allows us to say goodbye to Felix in the same part of the world where we first met him.

When writers start out, we're helpfully told that we need a lot of discipline because books don't write themselves.

Neither, it turns out, do they edit themselves, design themselves, publicise or market themselves, print, warehouse, distribute, sell, digitise, audio-record or translate themselves. Large numbers of talented and dedicated people make that happen.

To the angels at Penguin Random House in Australia, and at all the other publishing houses who keep Felix safe and healthy in their own various countries, my undying gratitude.

*Felix's stories come from my imagination, but also from a period of history that was all too real.*

*I couldn't have written any of these stories without first reading many books about the Holocaust and what came after and what still exists today.*

*Books that are full of the real voices of the people who lived and struggled and loved and faced death in that terrible time.*

*You can find details of this research listed on my website. I hope you get to delve into some of those books and help keep alive the memory of those people.*

*Their stories are the real stories.*

*Morris Gleitzman*
*June 2021*
*www.morrisgleitzman.com*

**The other books in the Once series . . .**

*Once I escaped from an orphanage to find Mum and Dad.*
*Once I saved a girl called Zelda from a burning house.*
*Once I made a Nazi with toothache laugh.*
*My name is Felix.*
*This is my story.*

'. . . moving, haunting and funny in almost equal measure, and
always gripping . . .'
*The Guardian*

'This is one of the most profoundly moving novels I have ever
read. Gleitzman at his very best has created one of the most
tender, endearing characters ever to grace the pages of a book.'
*Sunday Tasmanian*

'Painfully truthful'
*Sunday Times*

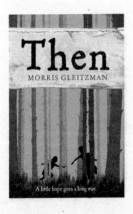

*I had a plan for me and Zelda.*
*Pretend to be someone else.*
*Find new parents.*
*Be safe forever.*
*Then the Nazis came.*

'. . . an exquisitely told, unflinching and courageous novel.'
*The Age*

'[Gleitzman] has accomplished something extraordinary,
presenting the best and the worst of humanity without stripping
his characters of dignity or his readers of hope.'
*The Guardian*

'One of the reasons this humane and carefully crafted book
is so readable is that the author celebrates ordinariness and
childishness even as he chronicles the terrible cruelty.
But prepare for shock and tears.'
*Sunday Times*

MORRIS GLEITZMAN

*After the Nazis took my parents I was scared.*
*After they killed my best friend I was angry.*
*After they ruined my thirteenth birthday I was determined.*
*To get to the forest.*
*To join forces with Gabriek and Yuli.*
*To be a family.*
*To defeat the Nazis after all.*

'Haunting . . . dangerous and desperate,
but also full of courage and hope.'
*Guardian*

'You will laugh . . . but not quite as much as you will cry.'
*Sunday Telegraph*

'Nail-biting . . . prepare for shock and tears.'
*Sunday Times*

*I hoped that soon the Nazis would be defeated.*
*And they were.*
*I hoped that soon the war would be over.*
*And it was.*
*I hoped that soon we would be safe.*
*But we aren't.*

'Extraordinary . . . one of the finest children's novels
of the past twenty-five years.'
*Sydney Morning Herald*

' . . . an awesomely epic adventure . . . It is the best book I have
ever read!'
*The Guardian*, young reviewer

'I'm crazy about this series. I recommend it to everyone I know –
young, old, teachers and reluctant readers.'
*Goodreads*

**BOOK OF THE YEAR – YOUNGER READERS**
**CHILDREN'S BOOK COUNCIL OF AUSTRALIA AWARDS**

18 May 1946

*Dear Zliv,*

*It's me you want, not Gabriek or Anya.*

*I caused your brother's death, just me.*

*But you'll have to come to the other side of the world*

*to kill me, because that's where I'm going.*

*If you don't believe me, check the newspapers.*

*Felix*

'This intensely affecting story will move readers of all ages.'
*LoveReading4Kids*

'*Maybe* and the others in the *Once* series are an essential read . . .
They are intelligent, clever, and action-packed.'
*Better Reading*

'Gleitzman tackles the post-war refugee movement with the
characteristic appeal of his series – all tales of adventure,
balancing tragedy and resilience.'
*Sydney Morning Herald*

**WINNER OF KOALA AND YABBA**
**CHILDREN'S CHOICE AWARDS**

*Once I didn't know about my grandfather Felix's scary childhood.*
*Then I found out what the Nazis did to his best friend Zelda.*
*Now I understand why Felix does the things he does.*
*At least he's got me.*
*My name is Zelda too.*
*This is our story.*

'One of Australia's, and now the world's, best-known and loved
children's authors, Morris Gleitzman tackles tough subjects
in a funny and offbeat way.'
*LoveReading4Kids*

'Gleitzman has a special way of seeing the world through the eyes
of a child, and generations of readers are grateful to him for it.'
*West Australian*

'Gleitzman's trademark fine balance of tragedy and comedy is as
sure as ever.'
*The Guardian*